~~Miss Birgit's Dilemma~~
Mail Order Bride

JULIETTE DOUGLAS

2017

Jared & Jerry

My sweethearts of the West!

Blessings!
Juliette Douglas

Copyright © 2017 Juliette Douglas
Miss Birgit's Dilemma: Mail Order Bride
By Juliette Douglas

ISBN-13: 978-1544091815
ISBN-10: 1544091818

ALL RIGHTS RESERVED

Editing: Debra Wagner
Cover: AmiLynn Hadley of Cover Design by Ami
(with RMJ Manuscript Service)
Interior Design: Rogena Mitchell-Jones
RMJ Manuscript Service — www.rogenamitchell.com

No part of this book may be reproduced in any form by photo-copying or by any electronic or mechanical means, including information storage or retrieval systems, without written permission from the copyright owner/author.

Contents

Chapter One 1

Chapter Two 7

Chapter Three 11

Chapter Four 15

Chapter Five 16

Chapter Six 19

Chapter Seven 30

Chapter Eight 32

Chapter Nine 44

Chapter Ten 46

Chapter Eleven 52

Chapter Twelve 56

Chapter Thirteen 69

Chapter Fourteen 74

Chapter Fifteen 78

Chapter Sixteen 89

Chapter Seventeen 95

Chapter Eighteen 100

Chapter Nineteen 107

Chapter Twenty 111

Chapter Twenty-One 123

Chapter Twenty-Two 128
Chapter Twenty-Three 131
Chapter Twenty-Four 137
Chapter Twenty-Five.. 139
Chapter Twenty-Six 142
About the Author... 149

Chapter One

Spring 1857

THREE TEAMS OF mules pulled the heavily laden freight wagon along a spindly, mushy stretch of road. *If one could call it a road,* thought Birgit Andersson. Sometimes it was lined with a brace of granite escarpment on one side and nothing on the other, scaring her half to death as she stared down the bottomless pit to her left. Other times they traveled through thick forest growth, the fresh scent of spruce and pine tickling her senses.

Mushy Drummond glanced furtively at his pale dark blonde passenger. *She's a game one…traveling by herself,* he thought.

He remembered how she had approached him at Mountain Valley stage depot and way station asking if he knew where Sinking Springs was and if he knew an Herr Johan Svensson. And…well…that was that.

She'd proved her mettle by taking over his cooking duties as they traveled further into the mountains. And a fine cook she was too, enjoying the meals the Miss ' had put together with game Drummond had killed along the trail.

Birgit no longer felt excited with the anticipation of beginning a new life. Traveling by train, then by stagecoach and now freight wagon, she just wanted to get to her new home. A Swedish mail order bride from Scandia, Minnesota, she was traveling to the heart of the interior western frontier in the Rocky Mountains. She had no idea what awaited her.

"Miss," the driver began. "Not much longer now…mebe 'nother day an' a haf…ta get to Sinking Springs." He glanced sideways at the young woman sitting tiredly on the bench seat. "I knows this has been hard on ya, but I kin see ye being a stout one and a beauty at that."

Blushing at the driver's comments, she answered in her soft Swedish accent, "Thank you, Herr Drummond, that was kind of you."

She never thought of herself as pretty. There were far more beautiful girls where she had called home. Birgit didn't have the flaxen hair or the fair complexion like other Swedish maidens, making her feel like an outcast amongst her own. And she was older than most, too.

"Ye be leaving family behind…" he questioned.

"No…no family," Birgit gave him a faint smile. Her mind wove through old memories of when she had been invited by another Swedish family to travel with them to America. Her heart yearning for adventure and excitement, Birgit wanted to see what this new America was like. Taking them up on their offer, she said goodbye to her parents, brothers and sisters. She sighed inwardly.

Has it really been ten years since I left Sweden? she asked herself, giving a slight shake of her head as she moved around on the hard bench seat trying to make herself more comfortable. It was no use; the wood still felt like she was sitting on a rock.

"Well...Johan Svensson is a good man...gits a might rowdy at times...but a good man ta have on yer side iffen trouble."

Birgit just nodded.

She had spent the last ten years of her life as a handmaiden to a local family in Scandia, eventually paying back her fare cost to the Swedish family she owed for the trip. Afterwards she was at liberty to begin saving any and all pennies she could. When Birgit felt she had enough, she took the plunge and began scouring ads in the local Swedish papers dreaming of becoming a mail order bride, finding that elusive love and happiness she yearned for. One day she found an advert from a Swede like herself looking for a mail order bride so she wrote to him, sending her letter to *Johan Svensson, General Delivery, Sinking Springs, Colorado.* After months of waiting and checking the postal boxes in the town mercantile daily, she had given up hope of ever receiving a reply. She wearily stepped up to her box one last time and peeked inside.

Miss Birgit's Dilemma: Mail Order Bride

A small gasp escaped her lips and grey eyes grew round staring at the rectangle of a battered oilpaper wrapped package held together with a thin strip of leather. Her heart fluttering uncontrollably, making her hand shake as her fingers reached, hesitated a moment, finally plucking the dingy stained package from the cubbyhole. Looking over her shoulder to see if anyone was watching, Birgit tucked it deeply within the folds of her cloak and quickly exited the mercantile.

Outside her footsteps picked up their pace until she was running to her favorite place in town, the livery. Pulling a side door open, entering and closing it behind her, she leaned against it to catch her breath, the pungent warm smells of the stable calming her slightly. When she had somewhat gathered her wits about her, Birgit scurried to the loft ladder, gathering her skirts as she climbed the steps nimbly. Only when she had settled down in the fragrant hay did she pull the letter out. Her hands gently caressed the oilpaper as something precious, fingering the odd leather tie instead of string.

Her heart just a thumping making it hard to catch her breath, Birgit slipped the leather off the package. The oilpaper crackled as she opened it further finding a neatly folded letter inside with a return address of General Delivery, Sinking Springs, Colorado. Lifting the pages gently to read, paper currency fell into her lap; she gasped.

Picking the bills up, Birgit stared blankly at them. *Forty dollars!* It had taken her years to save forty dollars and now she held the money as if she had found a gold mine. She cradled the currency against her breast as if holding a prized family heirloom and smiled.

Laying the money in her lap then settling deeper into the hay, Birgit began reading the letter from Johan Svensson.

Miss Andersson,

Someone is writing this for me, the same way he wrote the ads for the paper.

I ain't much on reading and writing, been a mountain man far too long. Don't know much else, except I can provide a good home for you and I'd be proud if you would be my wife.

Johan Svensson

X My mark

That's it? Birgit asked herself, turning the letter over then back again. She reread the neat script and smiled. Flopping back in the hay, she gave a huge sigh. Doubt kicked in causing her to abruptly sit up.

What have I done? she thought as her mind whirled with anxiety. *He can't read or write? Am I traveling west to marry a heathen? But he said he could provide a good home for me...what? A cave...a pit dug into the earth with canvas for a ceiling?* Her mind conjured up all kinds of scenarios causing her breathing to become short and shallow.

Miss Birgit's Dilemma: Mail Order Bride

She flopped back against the hay again closing her eyes and willing herself to calm down. Her insides felt as if she were churning buttermilk.

Another thought entered her mind. *I could just keep the money and not go…No…Johan sent the money in good faith, trusting I would come and be his wife.* Sighing deeply,

Birgit rose, shaking and brushing her cloak to rid the hay remaining on the clothing.

Straightening her shoulders, she marched the few paces to the ladder, landing one foot on a rung and began her descent to the dirt floor. Birgit Andersson strode purposely to the side door, opening and sliding through.

She was determined to make the best of her situation, packing what few belongings she had, buying her tickets and finally beginning her journey west into the unknown to become Johan Svensson's bride.

Chapter Two

SAWING ON THE reins, Mushy Drummond slowed the triple team to a trot guiding them to a stop in front of the one of the few buildings in the settlement of Sinking Springs. Wrapping the lines around the brake, Drummond stepped down. Looking at the woman, he drawled, "Be right back, Miss…gonna find some boys to begin unloading." He walked around the rear of the wagon into the store.

Heaving a huge sigh of relief, Birgit let her gaze roam over her new surroundings. The mountains lent a framed feeling nestling the little settlement within its hollow. Her eyes flowed upward following the mountain ridge with its granite peaks and the dark green of the pine and evergreens. New growth leaves tinted the lower elevations with spring like color. She breathed deeply of the crisp air, so unlike where she had come from. *The air back home…* she stopped her thoughts right there. Looking around again, Birgit smiled faintly, *No…this is home…now.*

Coming out of Trader Charley's Post, Mister Drummond walked toward her. "C'mon Miss…this

Miss Birgit's Dilemma: Mail Order Bride

here is yer stop," He held his hands up to guide her steps down from the height of the wagon seat. Settling her firmly on solid ground, he climbed aboard and retrieved her small worn carpetbag that held all her worldly possessions.

Taking her elbow, Drummond led her toward the steps and a wooden bench outside the store. Handing the bag to her, he cleared his throat, "Uh…Miss…does Johan know you were coming?"

Looking down at her hands gripping the worn handles of the bag so tightly her knuckles were white; Birgit shook her head, "No…" she said softly. Glancing up she explained, "I left as soon as I received his letter…"

Resettling his hat, Drummond pursed his lips, blowing. "Well…haf ta send someone up ta his place then…and let him know yure here." He moved toward the steps to go back to his freight wagon.

Touching his arm lightly, Birgit stopped Drummond. He glanced back at the woman.

"What's does Johan do?"

"You don't know?"

Shaking her head, Birgit explained, "His letter didn't say…it was short," she smiled.

"He's a mountain man…Miss. Trapper, hunter, tracker…and a damn fine one at that!"

Blinking, Birgit tried to wrap her mind around that. "Oh…" *I AM marrying a heathen,* she thought, sighing inwardly with unease.

Giving the woman a short glance, Drummond changed directions and entered the store again.

Grey eyes flicked over the small town, which consisted of three log buildings; the store where she stood, a livery with penned stock in a corral. The last building she saw had a crudely painted sign above it announcing: *The Lucky Strike.* Birgit didn't know what kind of merchandise that one might be selling. Turning she walked over to the plews tacked onto the wall of the store. Reaching out, she tentatively touched the fur. Surprised at how soft and thick it was, her fingers wove their way into the pelt, loving the luxurious feel against her hand. She continued to touch others, marveling at their softness.

***

"CHARLEY…" DRUMMOND BEGAN, pointing to the female standing outside the trading post doors. "…That woman out there may need some lookin' after…til we's kin get Johan down here…" he explained.

Trader Charley glanced at the woman then squinted at Drummond. "Hell fire…ya knows we ain't got no place to keep a wimman!"

Glancing around, Mushy turned back to Charley giving the shorter but stout Irishman a look, "Jus' giv' her some blankets and put her in a corner til Johan comes."

Charley gave Drummond a squirrelly look.

Miss Birgit's Dilemma: Mail Order Bride

"Where's yore squaw?"

"Got her out back working hides."

It was Mushy's turn to give Charley the squirrelly eye. "Well…this un is a lady…she don't know nuthin' 'bout our kinda livin'. But she's a Swede like Johan…so's reckon they'd be awright together…he'll teach her our ways or she'll die learnin' 'em."

Chapter Three

MESMERIZED BY THE furs, Birgit jumped when someone spoke softly in her ear. Turning, she blinked at the brazen closeness of the man in front of her. Her nose wrinkled as she caught scent of him.

"Youse be one mighty fine piece of wimminhood," he said as he reached for her. His pungent rancid taint came from one who bathes only on Christmas and Fourth of July, if then. Birgit held her breath as his odor swirled around her when she danced out of his way.

Birgit ran to her bag and held it up defensively in front of her as she whirled to face him. Her heart a thumping and cutting into her air supply, Birgit didn't know what she would do if he grabbed her. Grey eyes continued to assess the man in front of her. He was not much taller than her with his face covered in thick fur from winter's hibernation. Birgit wondered what lay under the beard. *Lice...or fleas...I bet...* she thought disgustedly.

Hazel eyes danced gleefully as he lewdly appraised the white woman. He stepped closer.

Miss Birgit's Dilemma: Mail Order Bride

"Aww...c'mon...I jes' want ta hold ya and smell that fine perfume ye's be awaring..."

Birgit's bag came flying up, whumping him alongside the head, surprising the hell out of the man and tumbling him sideways into what passed for a street.

She blinked, not knowing where that action had come from. Birgit stared at her bag, then back at the man in the mud. She struggled to breathe.

Flying out the door, Drummond stopped at the edge of the walk. "Randall...git yore carcass outta here! This here is Johan Svensson's bride!"

Randall slowly rose, rubbing his head. "Don't care...she ain't got no right to slug me..."

Trader Charley came to stand behind the thickset Drummond.

"Youse want I should tell Svensson...you accosted his bride?"

Randall shook his head briskly, already knowing about Svenssen's powerful swings.

"That's what I thought. She's spoke fer...she had every right to slug you! Now...git...for it's my turn or Svensson's!"

"What's you sticking up fer her anyways?"

"This lady is my responsibility until Svensson comes gits her...Now git!"

Walking toward *The Lucky Strike*, Randall glanced over his shoulder at the three of them standing in front of Charley's place. Giving a shrug, he pushed open the door of the saloon. He needed a drink. Guess he'd have to settle for his squaw smelling like bear grease instead of perfume which didn't set too well with him right now after getting a whiff of a pretty white woman.

Breathing deeply, Birgit tried to calm herself.

Turning, Drummond asked, "You okay…Miss?"

Nodding slowly, she whispered, "Yes."

"Miss…this here is Trader Charley…he'll look after youse til Johan comes and gits you."

Surprised, Birgit finally managed to get the words out. "But…but…how long will that take?"

"A week…mebe less…mebe more…."

Birgit gasped in dismay.

Thumbing over his shoulder, Drummond explained, "Johan lives way up in them mountains…"

Birgit glanced in the direction the thumb was pointing then refocused on the burly freight driver.

"…Got him a right purty spot too, but hit's aways off from here. He mebe out checking his trap lines or whatnot…so's it takes time to find him." He gazed at Birgit, "Livin's hard here Miss, but no place on Mother Earth like it. He was excited to be having a wife…so he'll come lickety-splittin' it outta them mountains ta claim ya," he finished.

Standing a little taller, Birgit stated firmly. "Herr Drummond, Johan Svensson will never claim me…"

Mushy and Trader Charley's eyes grew round.

"…I intend to be his equal in every way. I do not

intend to be his mistress or his slave. I came all this way to be his wife and a fine wife I shall be." With that she turned smartly, still clutching the worn carpetbag and marched through the door of Trader Charleys.

Four brows cocked as the men looked at each other.

Chapter Four

PULLING THE CLOAK tighter around her body, Birgit stared at the thick wet snow filling the deep wagon tracks and hoof prints in the sloppy street. She was used to surprise snowstorms; they sometimes appeared during the month of May in Minnesota.

Every day for the past ten days, Birgit would spend time standing, sitting or walking the one street waiting on Johan, wondering if and when he would come. She'd kept busy helping Trader Charley and his squaw with the store, but doubt had entered her thoughts and Birgit wondered more and more frequently if Johan had gotten word that she had arrived and had changed his mind. She prayed silently to God that all would work out and if it didn't? She had no idea what she would do if that were the case. *But when God closes one door…He opens another…*

Trying to keep her spirits and hopes high, Birgit pulled open the door and walked back into Trader Charley's store.

Chapter Five

RANGY AND LEAN, Packy Woods sat his dingy white mule, studying Johan Svensson's clearing. No smoke curled from the stone chimney. The only sounds he heard were a few chucklings and rustlings from the forest that surrounded him.

He hailed anyone within hearing distance and sniffed the air...*nothin'*...but it was still a might too quiet for him. He nudged the mule forward through the tall grasses and into the warm sunlight.

After helping to unload the freight wagon, Mushy Drummond found Woods in the *Lucky Strike* sending Packy into the mountains to bring Johan back to Sinking Springs and claim his mail order bride who had ridden into the spit-in-the-mud settlement with Drummond.

Packy never gave it a thought to get one of those mail order brides. Most mountain men like himself, would just buy or trade for an agreeable squaw from a local tribe for a few years to work their hides, companionship and such like. But if it worked out with Johan and his woman, he just might send for one, too.

A man gets mighty lonely hankering for a good woman sometimes, though in the past he'd had some decent squaws off and on for periods of times.

Maybe it's time for me to settle down wit a fine white woman, he sighed inwardly.

Re-focusing, he slipped off the saddle then dropped the reins, ground tying the mule. He squinted at the earth looking for sign in front of Svensson's cabin. A blade of grass bent here, a slight indentation there. But nothing showed to his experienced eye except days old sign. Looking up, Woods listened again. The quiet still prevailed as he walked towards the cabin's door.

Taking in the numerous plews draped over a railing, an eyebrow cocked as Packy thought, *Johan will bring in some good money for his new bride.*

Pulling on the leather strap that lifted the brace on the inside of the door, Woods entered. Gazing around at the small interior, everything was orderly. Sniffing, he smelled the old wood smoke and saw the ash dust that always littered a place from a constant fire. But this fire was cold, several days cold.

Hearing movement behind him, Packy spun thinking it was Johan; it wasn't. Stinky and Rocky came sniffling through the door.

"Aye…boys…I be lookin' fer Johan too," he said softly, reaching down and rubbing the backs of the raccoon and the skunk.

His moccasin clad feet walked silently across the

dirt floor and out the door, the raccoon and skunk following. Packy stopped and leaned against a porch pole, contemplating the situation. He knew Johan disappeared for several days at a time checking his trap lines and whatnot.

He had a partner, too; Micah Cunningham, a Scotch-Irishman who had linked up with Johan, sharing the cabin and sometimes trapping together. They were both pretty elusive once they got into the wilderness. And Packy knew from Drummond, Johan wasn't expecting a bride anytime soon.

So...

Eyes roamed the clearing, settling on the cache Johan built for storing his supplies. Sturdy logs held the cache six feet off the ground so wild critters couldn't get into it, especially when they came out of hibernation and were starving with hunger.

Reaching behind him, Packy closed the door as he spoke. "You boys keep a lookout fer Johan, now. His bride is in town 'n and waitin' on him."

Reaching for the mule's reins, Woods slipped easily into the leather. Nudging the mule forward, he began his search for Johan or Micah. He knew about where they might be. Rounding the cabin, Packy quickly disappeared into the thick growth.

Chapter Six

HEARING SHOUTS AND commotion from the muddy street, Trader Charley looked up from sorting furs and moved towards the door. Opening and stepping through, he walked to the edge of the covered porch. Honing in on Packy Woods, his eyes narrowed at the man's wild appearance.

A few folks surrounded the mule and the woodsman when he roughly slid the critter to a stop in front of Trader Charley. The mule heaved, coughed and hacked for more air after his harried run.

"What's got yure britches' in such a twist?" Trader Charley asked.

Flying off the leather, Packy scrambled up the steps to stand by Charley. "Johan…" he sucked in air. "Grizz got 'im…"

"You sure?"

"Uh-huh…"

Charley looked away. "Damn."

Both turned when a voice with a soft lilt asked. "What about Johan? Is he coming?"

After looking at each other, Charley broke the

Miss Birgit's Dilemma: Mail Order Bride

news. "Uh...no...Ma'am..."

Her stomach dropped to the the soles of her feet, thinking, *I came all this way...and now he doesn't want me...* Closing her eyes Birgit tried to remain calm, but her voice squeaked when she asked, "Why?"

"Uh...cause he's...well...he's daid..."

"Dead...?"

"Yessum..."

Birgit crumpled to the planked floor in a dead faint.

"Aww...dammit..." Charley muttered as he knelt by the still form. "Hep me move her inside," he told Packy.

Settling Birgit on her makeshift bed in the storeroom, the men stepped back, not sure what to do next. Spinning, Charley hurried a few paces, shoving the men crowding the doorway out of his path. They closed the gap again, staring at the pale unconscious woman lying on the furs, then their eyes flicked to Packy with questions mirrored in them.

"What happened, Packy?" one man finally asked. "Johan ain't no stranger ta the mountains...he knows its ways."

Shrugging, Packy replied, "All I's know is t'weren't much left of Johan when I found 'im."

"That ain't like Johan..." began another. "He knowed it's spring and them grizz'es apt ta be on thuh or'ney side..."

"What 'bout Micah? Find sign of him?" another asked.

"Nope...not a lick."

"Awright...ya buzzard baits...git on outta here...my Squaw 'ill take care of her!"

The men shifted letting Charley and Nona through. Staring thoughtfully for a few moments, she then briskly walked and knelt by the woman, feeling her forehead and taking a limp hand in hers.

Flapping his hands at the bystanders Charley ordered again. "Quit yure gawkin'...vamoose!"

Shuffling noises filled the quiet room as the men filed out the door then gathered on the porch. One leaned against a post taking the makings out of his pocket and began rolling a cigarette, transferring the pouch to the next man who repeated the process. Slowly, smoke surrounded the men on the porch as cigarettes were lit, the fragrant fog lifting to the rafters where it remained suspended against the wood before dissipating.

Puffing and squinting through his smoke, Whit Broadbent studied the news of Johan's death in his mind. His raspy voice finally broke the silence, "Peers we might have 'nother ol' Satan on 'r hands..."

The others turned slowly to stare at Broadbent, remembering the carnage of another grizzly not five years past causing shivers to walk down their spines.

Satan Three-Toes he'd been dubbed, one toe

missing and his prints so big, both feet of a man could stand within one paw. He wreaked havoc across the territory. Killing for the sheer meanness of it, not caring if it was human or animal, leaving the carcasses for the buzzards to find and the sun to bleach the bones. Satan was a smart grizzly too, springing every kind of trap set for him by man.

"Let's hope not..." one voiced. "He damn near stunted my growth by twenty years..."

Heads bobbed remembering the men they lost hunting the big grizzly and how he would always double back on them and quietly attack from behind.

"He even kilt that bar' man and his dogs..." one began then trailed off, looking at the others as if needing affirmation.

Some nodded in response, others stared up into the mountains, each remembering it all too vividly.

Packy stared at his worn knee-high moccasins then looked at the men in front of Trader Charley's store. "Best ta chust hunker down and see iffen thet bar' does it 'gain...we hain't seen hide 'nor hair of Ol' Satan going on five years now...so doubt it's him." His gaze traveled up the granite peaks. "Mebe a new young grizz, setting up his territory. Micah is still up thar...iffen he finds something else, he'll tell us when he comes down...he may find Johan's remains and he may not."

"You dinna bury him?"

"Under a pile of rocks..."

"What about Johan's bride?"

Packy shrugged looking over his shoulder at Trader Charley.

Charley echoed the shrug.

"Guess when Drummond returns, she'll go back wit him."

"I'd lay claim ta her…better than my ol' squaw any day…" He sneered lewdly.

Charley stepped forward. "Randall…she's a lady…youse ain't fittin' fer her like Johan wuz…you stick ta yer squaw."

Dirt crusted crows feet surrounding hazel eyes narrowed at the verbal insult.

Packy chimed in, "Don't even think 'bout it…Randall, you ain't deservin' of ah lady…like Charley said, you stick ta yer squaw…" he paused as a brow quirked up, then added, "Less'n…you be a wantin' ta brawl 'bout it…" letting the invite hang in the air.

A dozen eyes swiveled between Randall and Packy, waiting with anticipation.

Randall backed further into the street, whipping his knife from its sheath. "C'mon ya ol' stringbean…hain't got all day…" His eyes carried a hint of malice with the answered challenge.

Packy made clicking noises with his tongue against his teeth.

"Randall…you be dumber then a stump…taking on Packy," Whit Broadbent warned.

Miss Birgit's Dilemma: Mail Order Bride

Eyes flicked towards Broadbent then back to Packy still on the porch watching him. "He wanna fite ober the woman? I'll fite 'im...cause I mean to 'ave 'er."

More clicking sounds. Packy shook his head, eyes never leaving Randall as he took the steps, pulling his knife from its sheath, moving closer. "Cain't let ya ruin her...she's a good woman..." He began circling Randall.

Hilt gripped tightly, Randall waited for Packy to make the first lunge.

Hearing footsteps behind him, Trader Charley turned, seeing the woman leaning heavily against the door jam, Nona beside her. Taking in the pallor of her face making grey eyes huge, Charley said, "Miss...ya need to go back inside and rest."

Ignoring him and brushing stray tendrils of hair from her face, Birgit nodded towards the two circling in the mud. "What's going on?"

Looking over his shoulder, then back at her, Charley replied, "They's fite'n..."

"Why?"

"...Ober you..."

Puzzlement flickered through grey eyes. "Me...why?"

"Randall figures since Johan is daid...ye's up fer grabs and he aims ta 'ave ya...Packy's defending ya..."

Dark blonde brows crimped. "I'm not up for

grabs…as you put it, Herr Charley…I'll decide what happens to me." Birgit straightened her shoulders and stepped off the porch, picking up her skirts as she strode across the muddy ground.

"Miss…youse come back here! That's no place for a lady!" Charley ordered, following her down the steps, plucking at her arm. Birgit shook him off and marched onward.

One ear picking up Charley's warning to the woman, Packy's eyes remained on Randall.

Birgit came to stop a few feet from the men circling each other.

Glimpsing the woman and Charley in his peripheral vision, Packy ordered her, "Miss…git back ta thuh porch…Charley git her outta here…"

Placing hands on her hips Birgit glared at the three men.

Seeing that look, Charley remained off to the side.

Randall smiled wickedly knowing Packy was being distracted by the woman.

"Charley…git her outta here…"

The store keep lifted a foot to move, then stopped at the woman's reply.

"You will do no such thing…Herr Charley…" Birgit intoned. Focusing on the two men, knives drawn, "This is nonsense! I demand both of you stop!"

Randall tossed words, "I'll stop soon's as ya

Miss Birgit's Dilemma: Mail Order Bride

'gree ta be mah woman…"

"Like hell…" Packy said.

Birgit turned facing Packy. "I'll be the one who decides what is best for me…"

"Miss…li'ssen ta reas…" Packy's words cut off as he watched Randall lunge, one arm locking around Birgit's neck. She fought and screamed as the blade of his knife laid against creamy skin while he dragged her backwards.

"Y'all chust sit pretty now…me 'n mah new woman is gonna have a little get acquainted party…"

Whit had been moving nonchalantly around to the backside of Randall; with this new development he stepped up his pace. The butt of the Long Rifle smacked Randall at the base of his skull, crumpling him. The abrupt release of his arm about her throat had Birgit falling to her knees, gasping for air. Packy and Charley were at her side in an instant as their hands slid under her arms. They lifted Birgit to her feet and guided her to the porch steps. She collapsed on the top one, grateful to be out of harm's way and closed her eyes as her body sagged against a post.

After sticking Randall's knife in his belt, Whit motioned to a few men. "Boys…how 'bout packin' this flea-bitten cur off somewhere's…" Three men stepped forward, lifting and carrying the unconscious Randall soon disappearing behind the *Lucky Strike,* his home away from home.

Feeling a soft touch to her shoulder, Birgit

opened her eyes.

Nona stood there with a cup, silently urging Birgit to take it.

Nodding her thanks, Birgit wrapped still trembling hands around the tin cup, sipping gratefully of the cool, sweet water and sighed, thinking about her long journey and the strange occurrences of events since she had arrived. *I'm a widow...* she thought, *...before I was a wife...* tears spiked dark lashes; she quickly blinked them away. *What do I do now?* It was expensive coming all this way by the many modes of transportation she had to take and little money remained. Not nearly enough to travel back to Scandia, Minnesota, for sure.

Birgit looked up. Her eyes grazed the towering mountains nestling the little hamlet of Sinking Springs. They reminded her of the majestic mountains of her homeland. Suddenly she felt at home and knew she would stay. *But doing what? I have no husband...* A small idea began forming in her brain.

Looking over at the three men watching her carefully, Trader Charley, Packy and the one who knocked out the man accosting her, Birgit asked a question. "Do you know how Johan died?" Her eyes flicked from one man to the other as she waited for an answer.

Unease became evident as the three shuffled feet, their eyes touching on each others' faces before answering.

Miss Birgit's Dilemma: Mail Order Bride

Packy cleared his throat. "Uh…Miss…he was kilt by a silvertip…"

"A what?"

"A bar'…"

Confusion reigned across her face. "I don't understand…"

Opening his mouth to speak, Packy was stopped short by Charley ramming his elbow into his ribs.

"He means a grizzly bear…Miss…"

"Oh…like a black bear?"

"Three times as big and meaner…"

Grey eyes popped. "You mean you have bears that huge out here?"

"Yessum… 'n it being spring…they's real or'ney…"

" 'N obernoxious too…" Whit added.

Birgit frowned at the men's words, licking her lips thinking about what they had said about the bears.

Trader Charley broke into her thoughts saying, "It's chust best you stay wit me 'n my squaw until Mushy returns, then you hop on his freight wagon and head home…ain't nuttin' out here's fer ya anyways…now."

That brought Birgit to her feet, hands on her hips as she announced stubbornly. "I'm staying…"

"Miss…ya cain't…it's too wild fer a lady lak you 'round these parts…"

"I'm staying," she said firmly. Gesturing with her

arm, taking in the muddy street and the mountains surrounding the settlement, she looked back at the men with their gaping mouths. "This is my home now..." Pointing at Packy, "And you will take me to Johan's cabin..." Picking up her skirts, she took the first step.

Thumbing at his chest, Packy squeaked. "Me...? Aww...now Miss...thet place ain't fit fer a lady...'n...it's dangerous up thar!"

Turning halfway around, Birgit smiled. "Then you will stay and protect me..."

"Aww...now Miss..."

"...While I make that cabin into a home fit for a lady!" With that, she disappeared through the doors of Trader Charley's.

"Aww....hell..." muttered Charley.

Chapter Seven

STRIDING PURPOSELY TOWARDS Trader Charley, Birgit laid a paper on the counter. She turned it around and pushed it towards him saying, "Herr Charley...I will need these things to take to the cabin..." She smiled. "If you could please tell me how much all this will cost..."

Reading over the list, Charley's eyes grew bigger and bigger. Finally looking up, he stammered. "But...Miss...ain't no way in he..." stopping abruptly when he was about to say *hell,* he then rephrased. "We's...uh...well...we cain't get these things up here..."

Confusion marked Birgit's face as she stared at the shop keep. Her Swedish accent more pronounced due to her surprise, "Yes, you can," she stated firmly.

"A milk cow with calf...?"

"Would you not like fresh milk...butter...to sell...?

"...Chickens...rooster...goats and sheep?" Charley cried, his voice going shrill.

"...And wool...eggs...cheese...?"

"And a dog? But Miss…any stock you have will be killed off by mountain lions, wolves and such like…"

Ignoring his comment and planting hands firmly on her hips, Birgit glared at Charley.

He glared back, trying to reason with her, "Now Miss…I knows what I speak of…"

"I'm sure you do, Herr Charley, but this is my home, now…and nothing that you say or do will change my mind." Her finger tapped the list, "So…you best be seeing to filling my requests."

Rolling his eyes to the dusty cobweb draped beams above, Charley sighed, thinking, *Lord…hep me…she's gonna git herself killed up thar…*

Chapter Eight

SITTING ASTRIDE A roan mule with Packy leading the way on his dingy white one, Birgit and her entourage left Sinking Springs, heading deep into the mountains and Johan's cabin.

Chickens squawked, protesting in their cages that were roughly tied to the sides of pack mules. Bells clinked and bleats filled the air as a dog barked, herding the odd sight away from town.

People were shaking and scratching their heads, watching this oddity and mumbling, "She'll be back...yep, 'n high-tail it back ta where she came from...once she gits a taste of what its really like up thar...damn...fool woman..."

Oblivious to what anyone had said, Birgit marched determinedly on. With the help of Herr Woods, he insisted that she call him Packy, and a reluctant Trader Charley, she had surprisingly gathered almost everything that was on her list and made arrangements to pay off her remaining balance with goods for his store from her stock.

With the afternoon shadows deepening, Birgit

was becoming exhausted. She had never sat astride for this long, ever, that she could remember. The exciting adventure of traveling to her new home had worn off quickly as the day progressed. Now all she wanted to do was stop, eat and sleep.

"Packy? How much further?"

Hitching around in his saddle, he looked at her. "Aww…Miss…we's ain't even haf ways there, yet."

Groaning inwardly, Birgit responded. "Can we not stop for the night, now?"

Taking note of the fatigued face and slumping posture of the woman behind him, Packy gave some thought to her request, finally saying, "Iffen ya can hang on a few more hours…"

"A few more hours?" Birgit gasped. "I won't be able to walk!"

He smiled at her comment. "…There's good grazing and water for the stock, jus' ober thet ridge and down a bit…Miss…"

"Oh for heavens sake, Packy! Please drop the Miss and call me Birgit!" she said grouchily.

"Yessum…" hitching himself back around in the saddle and nudging his mule forward.

Taking a deep breath, Birgit did the same while scooting around on a boney back trying to find a more comfortable position; there wasn't one, prompting a weary sigh.

***

Miss Birgit's Dilemma: Mail Order Bride

FRITZ'S LOW, SOFT growl woke Packy and had him reaching for his long rifle. Sitting up, he tuned his ears to the forest that surrounded them, focusing his eyes past the low burning embers of the fire. He heard nothing, but something was close, Packy felt it as he lived and breathed. He quickly glanced over at his charge. Standing, he tread softly on moccasin-clad feet, until he stood over her body; she was sleeping soundly.

Fritz growled again, demanding his attention. Moving and squatting next to the dog, Packy laid a hand on the back of his neck, whispering in Fritz's ear. "What's out there boy?" Packy's first thought had been that it was a big cat after some easy fresh meat, but he hadn't heard a cat's signature scream alerting him. His second thought was another big grizzly was on the prowl nearby. Maybe the one that had killed Johan and that scared the bajeebus out of him. The old Satan had been sneakier and more dangerous than the average grizzly; it set his hair on end just thinking about the old bear. And with the stock and the woman, he wasn't real anxious to tackle any grizzly, if that was what was out there.

One last growl was uttered from Fritz before he bolted into the darkness. Packy heard the dog's body slam into something as more ferocious fighting filled the air, breaking the quiet. The woodsman tore into the brush after the dog.

Something invaded Birgit's deep sleep, causing

her to roll over and open her eyes. She gazed about the camp as she sat up and looked over at Packy's ground cover. *Empty!* That's when her ears registered the growling and fighting going on in the distance along with the frenzied bleats and frightened bawling. She froze, afraid to move as her breath wedged in her throat.

Inching closer, Packy watched bodies clash in the darkness. He couldn't quite make out the one shape just as yet, prompting him to silently edge closer, stopping when he heard a roar from about ten yards away. Fritz was fighting a bear.

"Damn…" he muttered. At that moment, he didn't know if firing over the bear's head would make him stop and turn tail to run or if he would have to attack the bear from behind with his knife. All he knew was he needed to save Fritz. It just took a few seconds in his mind, but to Packy it felt like hours. Raising the rifle to his shoulder, he knew he had to make good his one shot. Pulling the hammer back, he sighted in along the barrel. The bear swatted the dog away who yelped and lay whimpering, giving Packy a clear shot. He pulled the trigger; the bear roared one last time as it reeled back from the impact of the bullet and crumpled in its tracks. Packy's head dropped to his chest in relief. Standing, he ran the few short yards to Fritz, his fingers digging in the thick fur. Bringing his hand out, he stared at the blood covering his fingers. "Ah…boy…thet bar' raked ya good…"

Miss Birgit's Dilemma: Mail Order Bride

Scooping and gently cradling the dog in his arms, Packy picked up his rifle and made his way to their camp.

Walking through the undergrowth into the small clearing, the woodsman stopped in surprise. There stood the woman with a flaming stick in her hand walking back and forth near the now brightly burning fire, stabbing the air like a sword with it.

"Miss…"

Birgit whirled, grey eyes huge in a pale face lit by the flames, her hair taking on a golden sheen in the light.

His heart gave a lurch at her wholesome beauty even masked with fear. Swallowing he said, "Uh…Miss…"

Her eyes dropped from Packy's face to the dog he carried in his arms. "Oh…Fritz…" she whispered, dropping the stick and rushing across the distance to Packy's side. "Is he dead?"

"No…Ma'am…but he needs tendin' to…got raked by thet bar'," as he moved closer to the burning flames laying the dog down gently.

Gathering her skirts, Birgit knelt and cradled Fritz's head in her lap, softly stroking his head and ears. She looked up at the woodsman. "Can you help him?" she asked softly.

"Mebe…"

She watched as he took out his knife and began slicing the still wet, blood-matted fur away from the wound, exposing four deep gashes in Fritz's side. Birgit swallowed at the gruesome sight, but couldn't tear her eyes away watching Packy's hands as he deftly trimmed more fur away.

Looking up, Packy noticed for the first time a gentleness about the woman as she cradled the dog's head in her lap. His heart twitched in his chest watching her. When she glanced up for a few seconds, he dropped his eyes refocusing on saving Fritz. Laying his knife in the flames then glancing over at her as he cleared his throat making Birgit look up. "Uh…I gotta cauterize the wound…"

"What does that mean?"

"Uh…it means to seal it and stop the bleeding…"

"Oh…"

"…Then we gotta clean it real good."

"I thought you would do that first?"

"Naw…jus' the other way around."

"Oh…what do you want me to do?"

"Hold onto him tight…" placing a knee on the dog's shoulder. "He's gonna squirm hard when this blade touches his skin." Packy plucked the knife out of the fire waving it around to cool it some before touching the wound with it.

Wrapping her arms around the dog, Birgit squeezed tightly.

As Packy laid the blade against his skin, Fritz howled, struggling to flee the hot metal. The woodsman counted silently, *One…two* and lifted the blade

Miss Birgit's Dilemma: Mail Order Bride

placing it on another gash and repeating, *one...two...*

The stench of burning hair and flesh filled the air and Birgit's nose almost making her retch. Swallowing the bile in her throat, she concentrated on Fritz, trying to keep him still. She wanted to whisper calmly in his ear, but her heart was racing so hard she found it difficult to pull enough air into her lungs to even speak softly.

Finally, it was over.

After the dog quit struggling, Packy removed his knee from the dog's shoulder and patted him.

Birgit eased her hold, also giving a sigh of relief. She settled his head back into her lap, stroking his ears, chest and head, crooning to him, feeling Fritz relax as she did so.

Standing and sheathing his knife, Packy strode to his saddlebags where he squatted and removed a flask. Walking back to the prone dog and Birgit, he went down on one knee as the other was placed on Fritz's shoulder again. Unscrewing the cap, he gestured with the flask, "Hold him tight...this is gonna sting."

"What is it?"

"Whiskey," he replied simply, dribbling the amber liquid into the gashes.

The dog struggled, whimpering.

Birgit buried her face in his neck, speaking softly.

Removing his knee, Packy squatted back on his

heels rubbing Fritz's back. "That's all we can do for him now…" as he watched the woman lift her face from the dog's fur and look at him. He was surprised to see tears glistening softly on her cheeks.

Birgit nodded wordlessly.

Rising, he walked over to the coffee pot and poured two tin cups a little over half full, then he doctored the coffee with liberal amounts of whiskey in each and carried the cups back, handing one to the woman as he took a sip of his own.

Gratefully accepting the hot brew, Birgit immediately swallowed a mouthful, relishing the warmth as she closed her eyes savoring the coffee. Her eyes popped open as she choked and a violent coughing spasm racked her entire body.

Rushing to her side, Packy pounded her back until the coughing subsided. "Guess I put a little too much in your cup," he admitted guiltily.

Gasping for air, Birgit stared at him, demanding hoarsely, "Put a little too much of what…in my cup?"

"Whiskey."

"Oh…" she squeaked, clearing her throat.

"Thought ya might need something after all that…" tilting his head, gazing at her as he sat cross-legged across from her.

"Well…next time, just pour the whiskey in your own cup…not mine," Birgit replied rather firmly in her soft lilt.

A faint smile played along his lips amidst the

Miss Birgit's Dilemma: Mail Order Bride

thick stubble layering his lean cheeks as he dropped his eyes staring into his coffee. "Yessum…"

Silence reigned in the camp. Birgit took smaller sips of the laced coffee while she continued to run her fingers through Fritz's fur calming and relaxing him after his ordeal.

Breaking the silence, Packy blurted out. "We's got bar' meat ta eat and a good hide to work oncet I git it skinned…" he announced.

A frown marked her face.

He rambled on, "Gotta build a travois to put the hide and meat on along with Fritz…don't reckon he'll be able to walk fer a while…" his words trailed off embarrassed by her silence and confusion.

"Herr Packy…" Birgit began

"Jus' Packy…remember?"

She opened her mouth to speak, but Packy continued, "I ain't much on all thet…uh…whatchacallit…uh…fancy stuff."

Nodding, Birgit spoke softly, her Swedish lilt prominent, "Packy, I'm not used to the words you use or their meaning. Please explain…"

Enjoying the cadence in her voice he forgot to answer for a few seconds. "Uh…oh… 'bout what?" Nonchalantly, he reached for a few sticks of wood and added them to the fire, warding off more of the early summer nighttime chill.

"I mean the words you used to describe something. What's a trav…however you said it? Is it like a sled or something?"

"A trav-wah?"

"Yes! That's it! But what is it?"

Taking off his fur lined hat and scratching his head before replacing it, Packy nodded in agreement to her comment. "You're partly right. A travois is a drag sled pulled by dogs or horses." He took a slim stick and began drawing in the dirt between them.

Curiosity showed from grey eyes as Birgit watched Packy draw two angled straight lines with the top closer than at the bottom, making an open kind of V. He then drew an odd looking piece between the poles.

Lifting his eyes to look at Birgit, Packy explained, "Roving Indians..." seeing her perplexed look he rephrased, "Uh...Indians travel from their summer grounds to their winter grounds, instead of toting their belongings on their backs or carrying them, they made a travois and would harness it to dogs..." he nodded at the dog whose head was still in Birgit's lap. She continued to gently stroke the dog, watching him sleep.

"Much like Fritz here. When they tamed the horses they found runnin' wild on the plains, it made travelin' lots quicker, and a horse could pull more of a load."

Pointing at the drawing in the dirt, "How does it work? I mean...do you make some kind of basket between the poles to carry the belongings?"

Miss Birgit's Dilemma: Mail Order Bride

"Yep…" Standing, Packy commented, " 'N it'll make more sense oncet I git that bar' skinned 'n the meat packed away 'n you watch how I make it." He threw a look towards the eastern horizon noticing a slim line of color beginning to emerge, then shifted his eyes to the undergrowth. "I bes' be cracking…" flicking eyes back at the woman sitting on the ground with a sleeping dog in her lap. "You stay close to the fire and scream real loud if something approaches the camp…ya hear? Oncet it's daylight, I'll check the stock." As an afterthought, he added more wood to the fire.

Birgit nodded.

Looking around, Packy saw her blanket. Walking over and picking it up, he returned to the woman, placing it around her shoulders. Picking up his rifle, he disappeared into the dense woods without another word.

Gazing at the last spot she saw the woodsman when he vanished, Birgit absentmindedly pulled the blanket closer about her torso. She was surprised at how protective and caring he seemed to be towards her and especially Fritz.

She wondered if this was what love felt like. Smiling at herself for silly thoughts, her mind continued along those wanderings anyway. Birgit had never been in love and had no idea how it would feel. Right now the only feelings she had towards Packy was of the beholden kind. Her eyes drifted to the fading starlit sky as more color graced another day dawning. She sent a silent prayer. *Lord, if there is someone out there for me, I know you will show me...* She sighed, thinking the next words. *But if there is not, then give me the peace and strength to carry on, enjoying the life you have given me...Amen.*

Gently removing Fritz's head from her lap, she laid down with her arm as a pillow, covering both of them with the blanket and drifted off.

Chapter Nine

STAYING IN THE temporary camp another day enabled Packy to ready the bear meat for travel and build a travois to carry the load. The Miss had lost an ewe to the bear, which he skinned saving the meat and pelt, but the rest of her stock was okay after he spent half a day rounding them up. Those pesky goats were the problem; besides stinking to high heaven, they were always climbing on rocks and doing a stiff legged bounce dance across the terrain, bleating at him like they were playing a game of tag and he was IT.

Rolling his eyes and wiping the sweat from his brow, Packy sighed; never in his born days had he worked as hard as he did corralling the Miss' stock. The way he felt right now, farm animals were nothing but a pain in the butt with brains no bigger then a pine nut.

***

A DAY LATER as they continued to head in the direction of Johan's cabin, Packy reined in next to the Miss and called a halt. Heaving in a big breath, he gazed hard at her saying, "Miss…I ain't no mutton-puncher 'n I sure as hell…pardin me, Ma'am…ain't no cowman…but…them critters of yor'n has plumb tuckered out me and Spuds here…"

Frowning, Birgit replied, "But…but I thought you had everything under control…at least, you looked like you did."

Snorting, he answered. "Miss…ol' Spuds here is as crafty a mule as I know on these mountain trails…sure-footed…" Packy nodded towards her stock, "…as them goats of yor'n…but he don't know a lick 'bout herding farm stock."

Gazing around, Birgit sighed noisily. "So…what do we do now?"

Slipping off the leather and loosing the cinch, "We'll stop here for a breather…" Packy nodded at the dog on the travois. "Check on Fritz and eat a bite, then continue on."

Resting his arms on his saddle, he gazed at the woman who looked like she was hanging on to his every word. "One more night, Miss then we'll be there."

A smile burst forth like a ray of sunshine. "Thank heaven!!" she exclaimed, sliding off the back of the pack mule, trying to straighten her spine and walk normal.

Chapter Ten

REINING UP ON the edge of a clearing, Packy waited until the Birgit was alongside before speaking. "Well…Miss, this is it."

Her grey eyes roamed the small open meadow where a few patches of stubborn snow remained in shaded recesses and then rested on the cabin. She studied the ruggedly built four walls with the extended roof making a porch-like entrance to the door. She glanced at the many pelts hanging on a rail attached to a corner wall and post, with a few hides tacked onto the front side of the cabin and then swung her eyes around to a building on stilts with six steps leading to another small porch and door. Birgit watched the stock meander over to new grass and begin eating.

As the silence stretched, Packy began to panic. Clearing his throat caught the woman's attention. "Uh…Miss?"

After glancing at him, she averted her eyes from his questioning gaze. She continued to look over the small homestead, finally speaking in her soft lilt. "We have a lot of work to do, Herr Woods…"

Air expelled softly from pursed lips. Packy was afraid she'd want to head back down the mountain...*like now*... he thought. "It's Packy…Miss…"

She smiled then, thumping the ribs of the mule with her heels and moving further into the clearing towards the cabin. Packy followed obligingly.

Slipping stiffly from the bony-backed mule, Birgit's legs wobbled a bit before they felt strong enough to hold her. She sighed gratefully that the long trek up the mountain was over. Picking up her skirts, she marched determinedly towards the door.

Seeing that, Packy dropped the reins and ground tied his mule and sprinted after her. "Better let me, Miss…" reaching for the leather that would lift the wood latch inside. "…No tellin' what critters might have snuck in…" he explained.

Birgit shuffled her feet impatiently, anxious to see the inside of her new home.

Pushing open the door, Packy stepped inside followed closely by Birgit.

A putrid smell immediately assaulted her senses. Quickly pulling up her cloak, Birgit covered her nose and mouth exclaiming, "Ugh…what is that smell!"

Turning, Packy stared blankly at her. "Huh?"

"That smell!"

Sniffing the air, he proclaimed, "It's jus' the wood smoke…"

"I know what wood smoke smells like Packy! And that is not wood smoke!" Walking over to a

Miss Birgit's Dilemma: Mail Order Bride

boarded up window, she lifted the wood brace and pushed open the shutters, allowing light and air into the room. Spinning, she glared at the thin woodsman. "Something's dead in here and you had better find it…" Birgit threatened.

"But…Miss, I don't smell anything 'cept ashes and wood smoke…"

"…Probably because you can't smell anything but your own stench…" she alluded for the first time. "I'll wait outside while you find whatever is dead in here," making tracks back into the fresh air, inhaling a lungful.

Frowning, Packy took short whiffs of his person and clothes, making a face as he realized the Miss was right, he was a little rank. Scratching the thick stubble on his cheek, knowing it was still a might chilly to go dunking in one of the streams just yet, but he would once they warmed up some. Shrugging, he dropped those thoughts and concentrated on finding what was so offensive to the Miss' nose.

Tucking a few strands of dark blonde hair back into her braided bun at the nape of her neck, Birgit continued to scope out the homestead. *My own little farm…* she thought happily, smiling. Her mind began building the pens and where the barn would go and maybe a small garden? She had managed to squeeze some seed out of Trader Charley, but would have to check with Packy on what might grow out here. Turning to see what was taking him so long, something caught the corner of her eye. Focusing fully on the two critters with their noses pointing in her direction, sniffling curiously only a few feet away, her hand quickly stifled a scream as she took several steps back. She had heard the rumors associated with raccoons, you get bit, you die. Something called rabies. Now the skunk was a different story. She also heard once you got 'skunked' it took forever before the smell wore off. They kept advancing, little noses wiggling trying to figure out this new scent attached to the human. Birgit kept backing away, not knowing what to do. She had never encountered wild creatures before.

Lost in her thoughts, it never occurred to her to call out for Packy and warn him about the invaders. Feeling something tugging on her skirts, she looked down and screamed. Scared, the skunk whirled and shuffled as fast as its short legs could go to the far end hiding under the pelts.

The woodsman whirled, his arms loaded with furs and rushed to the door.

Birgit was dancing a jig trying to shake the raccoon from her skirt.

"Rocky! Cut it out!" Packy yelled, dropping the furs and reaching for the striped tailed bandit.

At the familiar voice, a black and white streaked head poked out from under the furs, eyes curious, nose twitching.

Continuing to back away, Birgit stumbled over

an unseen piece of wood, tripping and sat down hard with a whumph. "Oh!"

Carrying the raccoon, Packy strode over to the woman stretching out a hand to help her up. "Miss...Miss? You okay?"

Shying away, Birgit screeched, "Get that filthy creature away from me!"

Quickly retracting his hand, Packy straightened, cradling Rocky and rubbing his head calming him. "Aww...Miss...Rocky 'n Stinky won't hurt you. They's Johans'...he raised them from li'l bitty fellers. They's jus' looking fer him...missing 'im," he looked at her, mouth gaping while he continued to rub the raccoon. "They's hain't figured out yet that Johan ain't coming back." He offered his hand again and waited.

Still, Birgit hesitated. Her eyes darted from the woodsman's face to the shiny black eyes peering at her from his mask and back to Packy.

He smiled as his fingers gestured, "Once't ya gits ta know Rocky 'n Stinky...well...they's kin be a comfort..."

Reluctantly taking his hand, she retorted, "I don't think so..." brushing her cloak and skirt off. Gathering her composure again, Birgit honed in on the woodsman's face, folding her arms and sternly asking, "Did you find the dead animal?"

Letting Rocky scamper away, he straightened. "Uh...t'weren't a daid animal..." he nodded to the pile of furs laying a few paces away.

Birgit looked around him staring at the mound, then back at him.

"T'wuz them furs…Johan hadn't finished workin' them."

A dark blonde brow cocked up. "Anything else in there I should know about?"

Scratching his head, "Uh…don't think so…Miss…but than I ain't got the smeller youse got…"

Ducking her head so he wouldn't see her smile, she maneuvered around him, "Come along Packy, we have work to do…"

Rolling his eyes, he replied, "Yessum."

Picking up her skirts and stepping over the furs catching that awful whiff as she did so, Birgit walked through the door of the cabin again.

Chapter Eleven

SITTING ON A chunk of wood waiting to be split, Packy wiped the sweat from his brow and gazed around at the small homestead. There had been a lot accomplished in the last two weeks. The beginnings of a pole barn, several pens and a small garden planted with leftover seeds the Miss had wrung out of Trader Charley. He glanced at the roof of the cabin and shook his head, remembering how the Miss had made him dig bucketfuls of dirt and moss to spread on the shake shingles. Insulation, she had called it.

He'd known squaws that worked like beavers, but he'd never known a white woman who could work circles around a man like she did. Most nights he was asleep as soon as he finished supper.

Standing in the doorway, Birgit watched the woodsman sit on a stump with his hands dangling between his knees, head drooping in weariness as he took a break from chopping firewood. She smiled remembering the funny looks he gave her whenever she wanted something to be done, but in all fairness Packy did whatever she asked of him.

A shadow loomed in front of him causing him to look up. Birgit stood before him, a half smile lighting up her eyes, holding out a cup to him.

Taking the tin cup, he stared at the milky white contents then gazed at her. "Ya know…Miss, I ain't never drank so much milk or et so many eggs in my life til ya made me brung ya up here…"

Her smile grew broader. "It's good for you."

Draining the liquid, he passed the cup back to her. "Mebe…" Standing, he watched her step smartly back to the cabin, her skirt floating around her ankles from the motion as he sighed. Turning his attention to the task at hand, Packy retrieved the ax and setting a short log upright, he swung, splitting the wood in two. Preoccupied with thoughts of the Miss, he almost drove the ax into his foot a time or two. Aggravated with himself, he tossed the tool, gathered an arm full of wood and walked to the cabin.

Dumping his load by the fire, he straightened and looked around. The inside, though rough looking, now had a female's touch to it even with a dirt floor, but he liked the homey feel the Miss managed to create.

Raising her head, Birgit smiled. "Thank you, Herr Packy."

Giving a slight nod, his eyes watched slender fingers work the dough. Nerves had him clearing his throat and shuffling his feet.

Eyes lifted, then carried a perplexed look when

Miss Birgit's Dilemma: Mail Order Bride

he didn't speak.

"Uh...Miss..."

"Yes?"

"Uh...there's sumthing I's been meaning to ast you..."

Tilting her head, Birgit waited expectantly, fingers continuing to massage the bread.

"It's been on my mind for a few weeks now..."

"What?"

Embarrassed, Packy raked fingers through shoulder length dark hair. "Uh...awww...hell!" he exploded. "I'd be honored if you would be mah wife..."

Fingers stilled as a deep flush rose from her neck to her hair at his sudden announcement.

Packy plunged on breaking the deep silence. "We's work good together...and..."

Stunned, Birgit licked suddenly dry lips. Finally finding her voice she spoke softly, "I'm honored...but..." Her eyes grazed his face, "...Do you love me?"

"Love you? What's love got ta do wit this? We's good together...that's all that counts, ain't it?"

Closing her eyes, Birgit shook her head no. "It doesn't work that way, Herr Packy...at least I don't think it does."

Going on the defensive, eyes turning brittle at her remarks. "What's that s'pose ta mean? I'd make you a fine husband! Put food on the table...and take care of you like I have been...what more do ya want..." his words trailed off at her silence.

Birgit's face softened; she didn't how to break it gently to this kind man that she wasn't in love with him and never would be and would rather just remain friends.

Giving Birgit one last hard look knowing what her silence meant, Packy stormed out of the cabin.

Running to the door she called out to him, "Packy…wait…" but her words fell on deaf ears as she watched him stride out of sight.

Rising from his post, Fritz looked from Packy to Birgit, tilting his head when she spoke softly to him. "You're lucky you're not a human, Fritz…"

His tail wagged.

"Your life is so simple…"

Sitting, his tail thumped the ground in response.

Sighing, she turned and walked back into the cabin. She had to think how she wanted to explain her feelings to Packy without hurting him further. Picking up the dough, Birgit slammed it into the table and pummeled it with her fists.

Chapter Twelve

WALKING, LEADING HIS pack mules loaded with furs, Micah Cunningham was finally heading home. He still had plenty of work to do with the pelts before they would be ready for market, but he took pleasure in that. Micah wondered how Johan had fared.

Circling around and coming into the homestead from the southeast corner, he stopped abruptly and stared at the changes that had taken place in his absence.

Blue eyes squinted against the high noon cloudless sky under scraggly brown hair at the almost finished pole barn, a cow and calf with sheep and a few goats milling around and chickens clucking.

Micah frowned, wondering what had gotten into Johan going all homey like. Then he remembered. Johan had Trader Charley write an ad for him to place in several papers for a mail order bride.

His brow cocked, thinking, *Must've gotten a reply...*

Hearing hollering coming from his left, Micah turned and waited for Johan. As the dirty white mule came into sight along with the man guiding him pulling a log along a now muddy track, Micah blinked; it wasn't Johan but Packy. Ground tying his mules, he took steps towards his old friend.

Packy stopped abruptly, hauling back on the lines bringing the mule to a standstill as a smile busted out. Tossing the reins on the log, he trotted over to Micah taking the hand offered and pumped it hard enough to draw water. "Well...I'll be horn-swoggled! Ye gads man...'r you a sight fer sore eyes!" as he continued to vigorously shake Micah's hand.

Smiling at Packy's exuberance at seeing him, Micah slowly extracted his palm from the woodsman. "I never was before? What's different now?" he teased.

"Oh...lawdy...Mick...I hain't n'ber worked so hard in my life..." taking his sleeve and wiping his brow for emphasis.

"Prob'ly did ya good, Packy..." Mick replied, moving back towards his pack animals.

Following, Packy continued talking a blue streak. "...Naw...seen squaws work like thet, but n'ber a white woman ta work circles 'round me lak she does..."

"Who?"

Kneeling in front of the cold fireplace, Birgit kept at her task of cleaning old ashes from the hearth pit. Looking around, she realized the bucket was full. Sighing and standing, she pushed stray wisps of

Miss Birgit's Dilemma: Mail Order Bride

blonde hair from her cheeks leaving soot marks on her face. Wiping hands on her apron she left ash streaks there, too. Birgit picked up the container and marched to the door. "Packy..." she called.

Both men turned towards the voice.

Shading her eyes against the glare staring at the men for one or two moments she then said, "Packy...I need you to empty this bucket of ashes, please?"

Throwing out an automatic response, "Yessum..." Then nodding over his shoulder, "Thet...woman..." he told Micah.

Birgit gazed at the two men for a few seconds longer.

Opening her mouth to say something else, she changed her mind and clamped it shut as she observed the two men by one of the pens unloading pelts from pack mules.

Packy's chatter along with the quieter deeper tones of the tall one reached her ears. They had not seen another soul since their arrival to the cabin and now a stranger seemed to be making himself at home. Though by the sound of it, Packy knew the man. Curiosity had her stepping into the sunlight and making her way towards the men. Fritz followed.

Observing the female walking towards them, Micah threw his gaze back to Packy. "Who's she?"

Eyes going round, it dawned on Packy, Micah knew nothing of the latest turn of events. Harshly

P a g e | 58

whispering, "Ye gads…man! You don't know…do you?"

"Dammit…Packy…know what?"

"Thet's Johan's bride!"

"Ahhh…." Micah nodded in response. "Looks like I'll have to find a new place to sleep." Looking around, "Where's Johan?"

"Thet's thuh other part I gots ta tell ya…"

Micah's face showed confusion while he asked, "Tell me what…?"

The woodsman shuffled around refusing to look the swarthy man in the eye. Finally taking a large breath, Packy blurted out. "Aww…hell…Mick! Hain't no nice way a-tellin' ya this…but Johan got hissef kilt by a griz…"

"What?" Micah reared back in surprise at hearing the news.

"Uh-huh…"

"No way…Johan knows these mountains…where did you find him?"

"Up by thet stream ya call Clarks River…buried him under a pile of rocks."

Thinking back Micah nodded, "Yeah…that's where we parted company."

"Uh-huh…" Scratching his head, Packy squinted at the tall man. "…Some of them boys in Sinking Springs thinks it's a young griz marking its territory. Whit Broadbent thinks it's 'nother ol' Satan."

Lifting his eyes, Micah scanned the forest surrounding the homestead. "See any more sign?"

"Nope...but kilt a young brown bar' on the way up here...Fritz..."

"Who's Fritz?"

"The herd dog the Miss got...bar' raked him...but he's okay now."

"Whose idea was it to bring these animals up here? They ain't gonna last...it's a wonder ya got any left now."

"Hers...she shanghaied Trader Charley..."

"Well...that ain't hard," Micah grinned.

"Anyhoo... by the time me 'n Randall got through having a roustabout ober her..." Packy cut a glance at the big Scotch-Irishman. "Randall figured she wuz his prop'ty since Johan wuz daid..."

Micah snorted. "Randall ain't good fer nobody..." untying a pannier and propping it against rails.

"So's I was all set to fight Randall...then the Miss stepped in 'n tried to stop us..."

A dark brow cocked.

"...Yeah...she kin be a handful...don't li'ssen worth a lick...Randall snuck up on her, wrappin' his arm around her neck ready ta drag her off...But Whit Broadbent saw what was comin' and laid wood against Randall's skull."

"After that..." Waving an arm around, Packy rambled on, "... She made up her mind that this wuz her home now 'n..."

Micah's hands stilled, looking directly at the woodsman. "Her home?"

Packy prattled on, not hearing Micah's comment. "…She made me brung her up here… 'n well…plumb near worked me ta death…she has…"

He held up his hands, stopping the lanky man talking a blue streak. "Her home…?" Micah repeated. "…You know me and Johan staked a claim together on this parcel of land and it's ours!"

Packy blinked. "Uh…" scratching his head, then squinting against the sun as he stared at Micah. "…Uh…well…never got around ta telling the Miss that…"

"Dammit…Packy!"

Stopping ten feet away and placing hands on her hips, Birgit observed the backs of the two. Packy, lean almost scrawny compared to the wide shoulders that tapered to a neat waist and long legs of the other. "Herr Packy…?"

The soft lilt in the voice made both men turn abruptly, one looking sheepish and the other with anger glaring from blue eyes.

"Would you introduce me to our visitor?"

Micah gazed at the woman standing not far from them. He took note of the ash smudges on her cheeks and apron with tendrils of hair framing an oval face. A look of curiosity showed in her grey eyes and a slight upturn of her lips lent a hint of amusement to her fair features.

Miss Birgit's Dilemma: Mail Order Bride

Remembering manners he hadn't used in ages, Micah offered a greeting, "Miss…" dipping his head slightly.

Without thinking, Birgit bobbed a small curtsey. Her eyes remained fixated on the visitor as she canvassed him from head to toe. Shoulder length dark hair and scruffy beard hid most of his features except the blue eyes, which honed in on her harshly. Not sure of why he seemed to have such animosity towards her, she frowned. Glancing away from the stranger's scrutiny, Birgit stared at the odd-looking necklace around his throat. It looked like strands of thin leather braided and looped closely with some kind of ornaments strung together for decoration with strips of a red bandana woven within and about the strings.

A brow cocked when Birgit gave Micah a funny look after staring at his strange necklace.

Frowning, her eyes drifted south observing his red-checkered flannel shirt and leather-clad britches, noting the way the doeskin clung to his legs. She sipped air quietly as she licked suddenly dry lips, trying to calm her heart thumping against her rib cage. Birgit had never experienced that kind of wanton reaction before about a man and it stumped her, causing her face to abruptly bloom with color as she dropped her gaze.

"Miss…?"

Lifting her head, Birgit flicked a glance at

Packy.

"Uh...this here is Johan's pardner, Mick...uh... Micah Cunningham."

Birgit's breath caught hearing this news. "Partner?" her voice squeaked. "Herr Packy...you never said anything about Johan having a partner?" She swung her gaze back to the tall rugged looking man standing with a forearm leaning on the haunch of the mule, his blue eyes icy as a stream in winter.

Noting Micah's cold demeanor, a stubborn chin rose as she stated. "Welcome to my home, Herr Cunningham."

Straightening from the mule, Micah took steps towards her. As Fritz bounced up and growled, he glanced at the dog and stopped. "Your home?"

Arms crossed her torso against his frosty tone. "Yes...my home."

"Like hell!"

Birgit gasped. "Herr Cunningham...such language will not be tolerated!"

Waving an arm around, stepping closer to the Miss, he spoke through gritted teeth.

Fritz moved in front of Birgit and bared his teeth, adding another growl.

"Johan and I staked a claim on this land four years ago and as long as we kept provin' it up...it's ours...'n since he's dead...it's mine now!"

After looking around the homestead, Birgit allowed her eyes to focus on Micah. "I do be-

Miss Birgit's Dilemma: Mail Order Bride

lieve…Herr Cunningham…that since Herr Packy and I have already proved up the land more then you ever did…making it suitable for the animals and the fact I took that stinky despicable building you called home and made it livable again. And since it belonged to my betrothed…you are trespassing." she finished calmly.

Micah's gaze became thunderous. He moved closer, leaning threateningly towards her. The sound of more growls and Fritz's jaws snapping warnings mingled with his yelling, "Trespassing? Why you conniving…double-tongued female!"

Nervously, Packy kept shuffling around. Micah had a temper that wasn't easy to stop once he got going. He kept racking his brain on a way to defuse the situation; so far he was coming up empty.

Standing her ground, ignoring Micah's outburst, Birgit reached out to Fritz resting her hand on his back as she raised her chin in defiance. "You may have a rest for yourself and your animals overnight, then you will take your furs and whatever else is yours and leave tomorrow."

"Uh…Mick?"

Micah swung his head. "What?"

The way Micah ground out the word, Packy was reminded of a grizzly's low growl. "Uh…don't know thuh particulars of you 'n Johan's agreement…but peers the Miss could be part owner…after all t'was her ideas on provin' thuh place up…I jus' did the work. 'Sides youse was gone so long…didn't know if mebe youse was daid, too."

Birgit's smile was as wide as the stream at the bottom of the draw hearing Packy's words.

Micah paced off a few feet running his hands agitatedly through shoulder length brown hair, thinking.

Flicking a glance at the Miss, seeing her smile, Packy then glanced at Micah.

Spinning as his anger subsided, Micah looked at the cabin sprouting colorful wildflowers on the roof, the almost finished pole barn, the pens and small garden. He sighed; the Miss and Packy had proved up the place way more then he or Johan had ever thought of doing and it reminded him of the small farms in his homeland of Kentucky.

Walking towards the woman, stopping a few feet from her, he asked in a calmer voice, "And you are?" he asked as he ignored the dog's low rumbles.

Stiffening at his closeness, preparing to do battle if needed, she answered, "I am Birgit Andersson from Scandia, Minnesota." Glaring at Packy for not filling her in on all these developments, the woodsman flinched and looked away.

Micah asked, "So…you are Swedish like Johan?"

She nodded. "I am."

"And I s'pose you are staying?"

"I am," she declared firmly.

Sighing noisily, Micah stared at the ground and

Miss Birgit's Dilemma: Mail Order Bride

shook his head at her response.

Allowing her eyes to roam, Birgit took in the beauty that reminded her so much of her homeland. The granite-hued peaks, some with snow still on them. The strong scent of evergreens that filled her senses as she listened to the far off tap of a woodpecker in a tree, along with the sun-warmed breezes that softly caressed her face with its fingers.

Her gazed landed on the tall man and held his eyes. "I have come to love your mountains, Herr Cunningham..." she began. "...I answered Johan's ad, the next letter I received was his proposal and money to travel...I was so excited I never sent another reply...I just came. And now..." her arm stretched out as if gathering in the vista, clasping it in her palm and pressing it against her heart. "...And now, I am home," she finished softly.

Damn...

Studying her, his eyes slanted in thought, willing his brain to come up with a way to send her packing down the mountain, Micah said, "The winters are long and harsh here...Miss."

Placing her hands on her hips, Birgit countered. "Any harsher then the winters in Minnesota or Sweden?"

"Don't know, never been to those places. Your stock won't make it through the first snow...and..."

"They will if you and Herr Packy cut the grasses in that meadow," Birgit replied pointing to an area of waving grasses. "And store it in the barn...it will take several cuttings to have enough to get them through your harsh winters as you put it."

Looking over his shoulder to where she was pointing, he sighed as he glanced at Packy before turning to address her again.

Packy silently mouthed, *Told ya so...*

Micah threw a dirty look at his friend.

Packy ducked his head hiding the smile, scuffing the grass with the toe of his moccasin.

"That's a lot of work...Miss..."

"Ya...tis so..." Tilting her head as she gazed unsympathetically at the woodsman, Birgit challenged, "Are you afraid of hard work, Herr Cunningham?"

Micah bristled at her comment, his lips going into a thin line. "Miss...ye be a barking up the wrong tree...saying words like that."

Jutting out her chin in defiance, "Am I?"

Packy nervously shuffled around at the tense exchange going on, cutting swift glances at the two.

"You've gone plumb loco...thinking you can care for this stock and yourself wintering up here. You jus' have no idée how bad things can get...why...why you'd run outta firewood and th..."

"I have plowed through waist deep snow before...stringing a rope between house and barn to find my way during a blizzard...to do the milking..."

Micah continued talking over her words.

"...The snow will cover the cabin and the wolves

will be howling at your door...big cats, too...nope it's chust best you and your stock git back on down the mountain...afore it's too late."

Packy kept clicking his tongue against his teeth, the sound loud in the sudden silence.

Grey eyes sparkled with a hint of mirth. "Herr Cunningham? Are you through with trying to fill me with fear and send me packing, so that you can claim your land again and live like a heathen?"

"Heathen?" Micah spluttered. "Miss...you're the one with the hare-brained ideas of making this plot of land into a working homestead in this unforgiving country..." He watched that stubborn chin rise again.

"And so I shall...Herr Cunningham!"

Turning smartly, Birgit marched towards the cabin, head held high.

"Damn..." Micah muttered when Birgit was out of earshot. Scratching his head he glanced at the scrawny man beside him. "Now...what?"

"Told ya so..."

"Aww...shad-up ya ol' stringbean!"

Chuckling, Packy said, "Thuh Miss is hardheaded 'n stubborn as all git out, but I gots ta hand it to her, she's a worker... 'sides she's a mite as fine a cook as I's run across't."

"You jus' hain't no hep ah tall...no hep ah tall..." Micah fumed.

Chapter Thirteen

STANDING IN THE doorway, leaning against the jamb, Birgit looked through the darkness to where the two men sat within Packy's makeshift camp. The glow of a small fire sent orange and gold flickers of light across their features. At times, their quiet conversation floated through the crisp air reaching her ears. Pulling her shawl tighter around her shoulders warding off the chill, Birgit straightened and walked to the end of the dirt porch. Leaning against a rough-hewn fir post, her senses picked up the still sharp scent of pine as she looked at the looming thick canopy of stars overhead. She sighed. In her heart Birgit knew Micah Cunningham was right, that there was no way she could survive the winter by herself. *Why...I wouldn't even know how to fend off wolves, much less know how to handle a gun...* she thought, determined not to let Micah Cunningham realize how ill prepared she really was. She gazed at the stars again sending a silent prayer. *Lord...give me the strength to make it out here...please...*

Turning, Birgit called softly to Rocky and Stinky,

Miss Birgit's Dilemma: Mail Order Bride

waiting until they scampered through the door. Smiling, she had to admit Packy had been right. They were a comfort, sleeping on her feet at the foot of her bed every night now for the past few weeks. Bending, she gave Fritz his goodnight kiss on his forehead then stepped inside and closed the door against the darkness.

***

LIGHTLY TAPPING THE bowl of his pipe against a rock and knocking the burnt remains out, Micah opened a small leather pouch and pulled out fragrant shreds, refilling the bowl and tamping the tobacco into his pipe with a finger, then lighting it with a flaming stick from the fire. He squinted against the smoke curling past intense blue eyes as he observed Birgit at first standing in the doorway, the soft light of tallow candles behind her making a nice silhouette of her figure and then later as she moved to the edge of the overhang.

Not much could put Micah Cunningham in a lather; having battled grizzlies, mountain lions, Indians, men and whatever else that might cross his path looking to spoil his day. But the woman he met today, Birgit Andersson had him puzzled. He could understand if Johan was still alive, but to continue living in this place without a husband…that, he could not fathom. Leaning back against his gear and puffing leisurely on his pipe, Micah contemplated the woman further. Apparently, she was of the adventuresome sort. He wondered what she had left behind. Dredging up stories from the deep recesses of his mind, Micah remembered Johan telling him of the Swedish communities in Minnesota and how close knit they were. It confused him even more as to why she came all this way for really nothing, now that Johan was dead.

"Hain't that right…Mick?"

Realizing Packy had been talking a blue streak while his mind had been elsewhere, Micha looked at him. "Huh?"

"You ain't heerd a word I said, did ya…?"

Grinning around the pipe stem in his mouth Micah shrugged.

Packy shook his head disgustedly.

Removing the pipe from his lips, Micha gestured towards the now dark cabin with it. "Tell me about her…"

"Who?"

Rolling his eyes, Micah clarified. "The woman…"

Flicking his own eyes at the log structure then back to Micah. "Ain't much to tell…" Packy began, pouring another cup of coffee for himself and offering to fill Micah's too.

Micah shook his head no.

"She's got a kind spirit, saw that when Fritz got hurt and she's got sand…though…." Looking around, "I think living here will not be what she is expecting."

Miss Birgit's Dilemma: Mail Order Bride

Tapping the bowl against his hand, Micah tossed the burnt remains, listening.

"You et her cookin' tonight…"

Micah nodded.

"Best I ever et in a long while…"

Lighting his pipe again, Micah agreed with Packy's assessment of the woman's cooking.

"A while back…ast her ta marry me…"

A brow cocked up.

"Turned me down flatter than a wilted flapjack…"

Smoke spiraled into the air as a smile lit Micah's face, "Why?"

Shrugging, Packy replied, "Ast me if I loved her…"

"And…?"

"…Tol' her…what's love got ta do wit it…we's work good together…she still turned me down…just wanted ta be friends is how she put it."

Leaning forward, Micah removed the pipe from his mouth and gestured at Packy with it. "You been out in the woods too long…my friend."

"Huh?"

"A woman wants to know they are loved…" his mind searched for the next word. "Uh…cherished…if you will…"

"Huh?"

"Cared for…"

"Aww…hell…Mick…I care for her…"

"But not with love…"

"What's you gittin' so high 'n mighty on me for? You ain't got no experience, neither!"

Micah grinned. "No…but with that one I'd like a go at it…she's got spunk."

"Sheesh…you be as loco as she is sometimes…."

Watching Packy settle into his blankets for the night, Micah gazed at the log structure for a long time afterwards wondering what might lie in store for them.

Chapter Fourteen

HER NOSE WRINKLING at the odor floating across her face of the two men sitting in close proximity around the small table as they all ate the noon meal, Birgit pondered how she could convince them to bathe. When no idea of a bribe came forth in her mind, she decided an honest approach would be best. Birgit sighed loudly, dreading the resistance she knew was bound to come.

Micah and Packy looked up at the sound, then at each other and back to Birgit who silently continued to eat.

"Something bothering you, Miss?"

Looking up, Birgit shifted her glance from Packy to Micah. Laying her fork on her plate and resting her hands in her lap, she leaned back in the chair. "Yes."

"What?"

Her mind thinking on what to say, she stalled, taking a sip of coffee from her tin cup. She held the cup at chin level as if warding off the men's harsh retorts she knew would be coming after she said her piece. Birgit blurted out, "I can't take it anymore…"

Packy and Micah darted a glance at each other, their eyes lighting up and mirroring what the other was thinking. *Hallelujah! She's going back to Minnesota!*

"Oh…" Micah said, hardly able to disguise the pleasure in his voice.

"Yes. Neither of you will step forth into my home or take meals with me anymore until you both have bathed."

Micah's short temper rose at her comment, prompting him to slam his fork so hard onto his plate the food jumped.

Birgit's eyes grew round as saucers at his childish display.

Packy gasped, sucking a piece of meat wrongways down his windpipe sending him into a mighty coughing fit.

Plastering an innocent look on her face, Birgit gazed at the men. "Then I will give both of you long over-due haircuts."

Packy just coughed harder, face turning beet red.

Micah leaned forward menacingly, blue eyes hard and brittle. "Like hell…Miss…"

Her stomach wrapping into a tighter knot at Micah's fury, Birgit's stubbornness rose against his anger. "Herr Cunningham, ye be fixing your own meals if you continue to use such language…"

His coughing spasms easing, Packy sucked wind into his deflated lungs all the while flicking glances between the Miss and Micah wondering who was going to win this round. If he was a betting man, which he was, he'd lay odds hands down on the Miss.

Micah glared at her. "Miss…"

"Birgit…please…"

Ignoring her comment, Micah spurted, "…Iffen I wanted a nursemaid…I would'a gotten a squaw…"

"And lived happily ever after as a heathen," she saucily retorted. Grey eyes reminiscent of flint stared back continuing to challenge him.

Resting his elbows on the edge of the table, Packy buried his face in his hands, shaking his head at the exchange.

Fingers drumming agitatedly on the wood, his anger slowly easing, Micah glanced briefly at Packy who still had his head buried in his hands. He looked at Birgit, studying the proud chin, the flint in her eyes carrying a strength and determination he was not used to witnessing in these rugged mountains. White women were still few and far between out here.

Realizing no further confrontation was coming, Birgit squared her shoulders; when she pushed back her chair it scraped tracks into the dirt floor. Standing, she made motions of picking up the tin plate when she heard Micah clear his throat. Looking calmly at him, she waited for him to speak.

Micah chewed on the ends of his overhanging moustache, stalling.

Tilting her head, she prompted, "Yes?"

"Uh…well, we kinda have to do things differently out here than back east."

Birgit waited.

Packy looked up, wondering how deep of a hole Micah was going to dig this time.

"Well…ya see the less bathing we do, the less the bugs bother us and such…" Looking at Packy for help.

Packy just rolled his eyes leaving them focused on the shingled ceiling refusing to look at either of them.

Keeping her face deadpan at his lying comment, Birgit picked up her plate, spinning and throwing the words over her shoulder as she walked out the door to feed Fritz. "Ya…tis true…but so does cleanliness, Herr Cunningham…so does cleanliness…"

Chapter Fifteen

"DAMN…WOMAN…" MUTTERED Micah as he and Packy reluctantly headed down the gently graded slope through the tall grasses of a small meadow towards the stream doing as Birgit ordered: to bathe or be cut off from her good meals. Something he wasn't ready to give up just yet, Micah realized.

Ignoring Micah's mumblings and sniffing the bar of homemade soap Birgit had made recently, Packy said, "Hey, this smells purty good!" shoving the light tan bar under Micah's nose.

Pushing Packy's arm away, Micha groused, "Aww…shad-up ya dried up strip of buffalo hide!"

Chuckling, the scrawny woodsman ribbed him some more. "Mick…youse jus' sore cause she bested ya a'gin…"

Micah threw him a dirty look as he pulled up at the stream and stared at the sunlit sparkling water. He sighed, knowing it would still be cold.

Squatting on the sloping bank, Packy dipped his hand in the water, swirling it around. "Ye…gads! We's gonna freeze 'r arses off…"

Juliette Douglas

Sitting in the thick grass at the stream's edge, Micah began unlacing his knee high moccasins. Lifting a leg and grabbing an ankle, he pulled the leather off his foot, repeating with his left. Setting them aside, he stared at his grimy feet, grimacing at the ground in dirt he saw caking his toes and ankles.

Standing, he reached for the bar of soap and took a step staring at the water. A shiver ran down his backbone just thinking of bathing in that chilling snow melt water.

"You hain't really gonna do it…'r ya?"

Darting a glance at Packy, "You wanna keep eatin' her fine cookin'?" Micah asked. "You'll do it." Taking a deep breath, he plunged into the icy stream, Packy sighed deeply before doing the same.

***

HUMMING A LONG ago forgotten tune that popped into her head, Birgit took the bucket to fill from the spring behind the cabin so the men could shave when they finished bathing. As she walked, she marveled at how the farm was coming together in the last month and a half since she and Packy had arrived.

Standing quietly, she let the sounds of forest and farm wash over her ears. The soft clucking of the chickens, short bleats from the sheep and goats. Occasional blowing from the mules as they and the cow and calf softly munched on the thick grasses. Hearing a hawk's cry, she looked up, her hand shielding her eyes from the bright sun and watched it soar across the treetops towards the stream.

Closing her eyes, she breathed deeply of the sun-warmed air allowing her senses to pick out the earthly scents. The dank mustiness of a layered carpet under hardwoods and pines from years of shedding their summer coats now providing a rich soil for new growth to thrive in. The light perfume of wildflowers and the stronger aroma of pine teased her nose. Her ears picked out the slight scurrying of small forest creatures along with their chatter and a woodpecker doing his constant tap-tap against the trees.

Opening her eyes Birgit sighed gratefully, glad that she had taken this journey, even though it had left her a widow before she was a bride and still had no idea what lay in store for her future.

Looking up she whispered, "Thank you, Lord…"

Soon she and Packy would need to make a trip to Sinking Springs as she would have enough goods to pay off her debt and trade for more items with Charley in his store. Birgit sighed happily with that knowledge. But now her steps slowed as she paused in her thoughts, thinking of the rough woodsman, Micah with his dark hair and fierce blue eyes.

She was unsure as to where she really stood with him. He was quick to temper but then seemed to get over it just as fast. He wasn't as easy to read as the amicable Packy nor as much fun, but still tolerable.

Watching Fritz scamper into the brush following

a scent, Birgit smiled as she continued to walk towards the small cache Packy had built her to store her milk, butter and cheese in keeping them cool over the spring.

Dipping the bucket into the water filling it, she set it aside and took the dipper from a nail on the side of the cache for a drink. The sweet tasting liquid slid down her throat refreshingly. Hanging the dipper in its place, Birgit picked up the bucket and started back towards the cabin.

***

FINGERS AND LIPS blue, Packy and Micah finally felt they had scrubbed their clothes and bodies squeaky-clean enough to satisfy Miss Fancy-pants, they hoped as they gratefully stepped out of the icy water onto the grassy bank.

Removing his red flannel shirt, Micah wrung the excess water out of it, shook the material and laid it on the grass. Fingers ran through his hair as he tried to make some kind of order out of the sopping mess. Then he sat and lay back, savoring the warmth of the ground against his chilled skin, closing his eyes.

***

COMING AROUND THE side of the cabin, Birgit pulled up abruptly seeing who was in her front yard. Sitting on four ponies riding bareback were Indians staring at her. Long black –brown hair either braided or hanging loose draped across their doeskin garments. Bows and quivers were strapped to their backs with one carrying a long rifle positioned across his knees as he sat his horse, shot and powder horn slung from one shoulder.

At first, surprise rendered Birgit speechless: then fear overtook her as the bucket slipped from her fingers, its contents soaking her dress and the ground as she screamed and took off running back towards the spring. Her mind was befuddled as to what she should do.

A guttural grunt came from one as he hopped off his pony and gave chase. Catching Birgit, she screamed louder as the Indian dragged her fighting and lashing out at him back to the front of the cabin. His fingers were biting into her arms so tightly; Birgit could feel them bruising her upper arms. The brave positioned her in front of their leader and said some foreign gibberish to her ears. She screamed again, continuing to fight the man holding her.

Fritz came flying out of the brush, and attacked the heathen holding his mistress causing him to release her.

Hearing the screams, Micah and Packy rose instantly, trying to run and put their footgear back on their feet at the same time.

Falling to the ground, Birgit watched the brave whirl and pull his knife and face a growling, snapping Fritz.

His lunge at the dog had Birgit bouncing up crying "No…" as she shoved him away from Fritz causing him to lose his balance, tumbling and rolling.

She raced to the dog's side, wrapping her arms around his neck as Fritz continued to threaten anyone who wanted to harm her by growling low in his throat. Birgit darted frightened glances at the brave slowly rising and the other three who remained on their horses watching all this unfold. She tried to pull air back into her lungs, but it was impossible; her heart banged what little she managed to breathe in, out.

Topping the short rise, Packy on his heels, Micah slowed recognizing the four braves calling out, "Welcome…my brothers…"

Four heads swiveled at his voice.

Birgit's eyes already round as wagon wheels from fear grew larger with the fact that Micah seemed to know these strange red men.

Taking stock of the situation, Micah knew what he had to do; he didn't want to…but had to. Reaching Birgit, he pulled her to her feet and pulled her in close.

Her eyes silently questioned his motives as her fingers pushed against his naked chest in resistance.

His lips took hers. Birgit gasped against him trying to pull away; he held her tighter, one hand bracing the back of her head against his lips curtailing her squirming. Parting them with his tongue, Micah tasted her warm sweetness surprising him at how much he enjoyed the quick kiss.

His beard was scratchy against her skin and tickled her nose, Birgit tried to push herself away once again. Releasing her mouth, his lips slid across her cheek to rest near her ear.

Micah whispered a harsh warning. "You follow my lead or you'll be going home with them to be their squaw…"

Birgit sucked in a short breath of air at his words, her eyes darting in the direction of the Indians then flicking them away from the braves' intense study of her just as quick.

"…'n don't give me no sass neither…" With that Micah released her and turned Birgit and himself to face the four on horseback.

Managing to finally put the doeskin back on his feet, Packy waited to see what would transpire next. The Miss was a handsome woman and any brave would be proud to have her as his squaw.

Micah hissed, "Put your arm around my waist…and try to look as if ya might kinda like me…"

Hearing his words, Birgit opened her mouth to say something, but Micah's threatening glance had her clamping it shut. She did as she was told, giving him a weak counterfeit smile. Then her eyes settled on the four horsemen.

The apparent leader addressed Micah in English.

"Touch The Sky…"

Birgit blinked, cutting a curious look at the tall woodsman standing confidently next to her wondering about the Indian's words and their meaning, *Touch The Sky*.

"Welcome…" Micah began, "Spotted Wolf…what brings you here today?"

Packy moseyed to stand next to Micah. He knew the four horsemen were more of a hunting party than a warring faction.

Birgit chewed on her bottom lip fascinated but scared to death at the same time with the visitors.

Pointing, Spotted Wolf gestured to Micah then to Birgit. "Touch The Sky…your squaw?"

"Yes." Squeezing Birgit in closer to his side.

Spotted Wolf grunted. Birgit went to studying the ground and the tips of her soiled shoes peeking out from under her dress unnerved at the feelings she was having being scrunched up against Micah's naked torso. Her nose caught a whiff of fresh soap along with her skirt becoming wet from his leather britches.

She sipped air trying to calm her heart beating a drum roll against her ribs as she cut a look towards their visitors wondering about them. A deadpan look remaining on his face, Packy continued to observe the men waiting, for what he did not know. Most times a hunting party was peaceable unless provoked.

The silence stretched, interrupted only by the ponies' tails swishing and hooves stamping occasionally, mingled with the soft clucking and bleats coming from the pens.

Micah opened his mouth to finally break the silence, but was cut short by Spotted Wolf saying, "Big bear...two suns..." pointing towards the northeast.

Packy and Micah looked at each other.

"...Many sign...fresh kills..."

Micah signed. *Three-Toes?*

Shaking his head no, Spotted Wolf added, "Young, big...angry..."

"Might been the one got Johan...Mick..."

Micah nodded. Breaking away from Birgit, he walked over to Spotted Wolf. "Thank you my brother...we will keep watch."

Giving a short nod, the hunting party whirled their horses and headed down the slope to the stream.

Birgit came to stand next to Micah. "What did he mean?"

"Means we gotta big griz to watch out for..." He glanced at her. "Now's the time for you to start gathering your things. Packy will take you and your stock back to Sinking Springs."

Straightening her spine, Birgit stated firmly, "I'll not go."

"Birgit..." using her name for the first time. "You ain't safe here..."

"Oh? And you think I'll be safer on a wide open trail than here?" Her arm gestured at the cabin.

Following her arm, Micah looked at the small

house a few moments before returning his attention to her adding, "A big griz would make kindling sticks outta that cabin."

Placing hands on her hips, Birgit turned and studied the building. "Well…then, Fritz and I will just climb on the roof and wait until the bear is gone."

Micah snorted. "Like…hell! If you think being up there is gonna keep you safe?!"

"Miss…"

Birgit's head swiveled looking at Packy.

"…This time Mick is right…"

Micah threw Packy *the* look at his comment.

Ignoring the man, Packy continued, "…Hain't gonna be safe for you up here…leastways…till that critter is gone or daid, one… 'n we's don't know when that might rightly be…so…"

"I'm staying."

"Confound it…you stubborn woman!!" Micah yelled. "Can't you see we're trying to keep you safe?!"

Marching smartly up to Micah, Birgit slapped him so hard his head swiveled.

Packy's eyes went round as a tree stump. Rubbing his face Micah splurted, "What the hell did you do that for?"

"That, Herr Cunningham, was for kissing me and trying to still get me off my land!" She spit out angrily as she spun and began walking briskly back to the cabin.

Miss Birgit's Dilemma: Mail Order Bride

Sprinting, Micah caught her elbow spinning Birgit around, gripping both arms tightly.

"Ow…let me go…you're hurting me."

"Dammit woman…" Micah hissed. "When those braves saw you…the first thought running through their minds was to capture you and turn you into one of their squaws! I did what I had to, to save you! Ungrateful…wench!"

Her struggling abruptly stopped at the words *ungrateful wench*.

"How dare you use such…such…despicable words against me?" Birgit peeled his calloused fingers from her arms. Her hand rose to slap him again, but Micah was quicker, grasping her wrist.

"Woman! You are the most stubborn…contrary…and hard-headed female I ever…ever did run across't!" he shouted.

Jerking her wrist out of his grip, grey eyes glared at him, then she whirled and finished marching to the cabin slamming the door with a bang only to have it swing open again. Packy and Micah watched it close more softly this time. The two looked at each other with Packy scratching his head at the turn of events. Micah turned and stomped towards the stream to retrieve his shirt.

Chapter Sixteen

"HI-LO…" JAMES LAVANIER hailed as he approached the homestead. Slowing and stopping twenty feet from the cabin he looked around, puzzled at what greeted his eyes. Sheep, goats, mules in a fenced area, a barn going up and chickens clucking in the yard interrupted the peaceful quiet. He called out louder, "Johan? Mick? Anybody home?"

Hearing the voice a second time, Birgit wondered who would be this far out. She pushed back a stray tendril of hair from her face and opened the door a crack. After the Indians, she practiced more caution. All she saw was another mountain man, darker this time with pelt-loaded mules. Opening the door wider she stepped out, wiping her hands on her apron nervously. Not knowing what to expect, she stayed close to the door.

Catching movement out of the corner of his eye, James turned, ebony eyes going wide at the blonde woman standing under the overhang. Ground tying his mules, James took a few paces towards her. Noticing how she backed against the doorjamb, he stopped

Miss Birgit's Dilemma: Mail Order Bride

his forward movement, asking, "Miss…is Johan here?"

Birgit remained silent, her gaze taking stock of the man twelve feet in front of her, his ebony skin glistening with sweat from the overly warm day.

"Miss…?"

Swallowing, she questioned, "Who are you?"

"A friend of Johan and Mick…Ma'am…James Lavanier."

"Oh…" her eyes drifted from him to the barn. "The men are over there…" Birgit swiftly stepped inside and closed the door, latching it. She leaned against the wood sighing with relief. Then noticing the windows open, she quickly closed the open windows and put the crossbar in place, plunging the room into darkness with only the fire in the hearth throwing out light.

Frowning and puzzled by the woman's odd reception, James focused on pulling his mules over to the fence and removing the panniers and pelts giving the animals a break. Looking and finding the gate, he opened and strode through. Walking several yards, now he could hear voices coming from the backside of the barn. Rounding the corner, James stood quietly, big grin spreading across his face.

Feeling a presence, Micah looked up and smiled seeing James. He punched Packy, pointing.

Looking over his shoulder, Packy exclaimed, "Well…well…if it ain't ol James Lavanier!"

"Howdy…boys…" stepping forward and taking the hands offered. Looking around, James asked, "What the hell got into you two and Johan…"

"Uh…well…"

"…And who's that woman back there…"

Micah spoke first. "That was Johan's mail order bride…"

"Well…I'll be…went and got hisself hitched…huh?" Then it dawned on James. "Wait…did I hear you say 'wuz'…"

"Uh-huh…"

Resting the butt of his long rifle on the ground, both hands wrapped around the barrel as James stared over the muzzle at the two men. "Well…spit it out, man!"

"See any griz sign on your way here?" Micah asked.

Ebony eyes narrowed at the switch in conversation. "Yeah…two days out…but ya still ain't tol me what's going on here…"

Micah and Packy turned back to tapping wood chinks between the logs not answering James.

Becoming frustrated, James demanded, "Where's Johan?"

"Johan's daid…" Packy admitted simply. Turning to James he further explained, "Thet woman up thar came all thuh way from Minnesota ta be his bride, but somewhere's between her travelin' 'n gittin' here, a griz got Johan."

Miss Birgit's Dilemma: Mall Order Bride

"Damn..." exclaimed James softly.

"I found his tore up body back on Clarks River."

More interested in where the grizzly was at the moment instead of the retelling of Johan's death, Micah asked James. "Which way was that griz sign heading..."

Dark eyes bored into Micah's face. "What you keep changing the subject here for?"

"Cause iffen we's got trouble I want a heads up on it," Micah defended then added, "On account of her..."

Packy grinned, directing his words at James giving a wink. "Mick here...he kinda likes her..."

The large muscular colored mountain man smiled.

"Watch yer mouth...man...I do not like her...she's contrary... 'n...stubborn as all get out."

Chuckling, Packy replied, "Uh-huh..."

Micah shook his head in disgust.

"So..." James began, "...Why the stock and this barn? Ain't nuthin' gonna make it through these winters..."

"Oh...Mick and the Miss got a feud goin' on...'bout thet."

"Huh?"

"Packy...you jus' don't know when ta shadup...do you?"

"Why...Mick...I's just filling ol James here in...is all... 'sides we could use all the hep we can with the work the Miss has all lined up for us ta do afore winter sets in."

Micah rolled his eyes.

James gave a big toothy smile.

A loud banging reached their ears.

"That's the dinner bell," Packy said. "And I'm starving!"

The three walked through the now tramped down barn lot on the way to the cabin. Micah asked James, "Where'd you winter up?"

"Arapaho camp."

Nodding, Micah revealed, "Spotted Wolf stopped by a few days ago to tell us 'bout the griz sign..."

Seeing the three men heading in her direction, Birgit sighed thinking, *Another friend...* as she stepped inside to set another plate. *Way out here in these woods and I've seen more people then I ever thought I would.* As she waited on the men, she realized that if she didn't remind them to wash up before meals, they wouldn't.

Stepping under the overhang, Packy started to make introductions, "Uh...Miss, this here is a friend of our'n...James L..."

Giving a curt nod in greeting, "We've met..."

"Uh...James, this here is Miss Birgit Andersson."

"Howdy...Ma'am."

"Well...wash up first..." and with those words Birgit turned on her toes and walked back into the cabin.

James cocked a brow, questioning.

Washing up, Packy gave James a piece of advice. "Now…James, the Miss is a mighty fine cook but don't be none too surprised if she hands you a bar of soap and tells ya ta go down to the stream and take a bath…"

"What?"

Micah snorted.

Continuing, Packy nodded. "…Uh-huh…according to her…cleanliness is next to Godliness…" he warned as the three men trouped in for dinner.

Chapter Seventeen

LISTENING IDLY TO the conversation swirling around her from the three men bantering back and forth made Birgit feel even lonelier.

She had nothing in common with these men and that niggling thought in the back of her mind kept popping up, *Maybe I did make a mistake staying...*

Birgit didn't know if things would have been different if Johan had still been alive or not.

She liked Packy, despised Micah, and was leery of James, though she had no reason to be.

She scolded herself, *Stop it...Packy and Micah trust him and I should be able to do that, too...*

Watching Birgit out of the corner of his eye while conversing with James and Packy, Micah noticed she was just pushing the food around on her plate and not eating.

He watched as she laid the fork down on the plate, pushed back her chair and rose carrying the plate disappearing out the door.

James and Packy fell silent seeing her go, then looked at Micah with questioning glances.

Miss Birgit's Dilemma: Mail Order Bride

Catching that, the tall woodsman shrugged, picking up his coffee and took a sip. A few moments later, Micah rose from the bench seat and strode out the door after Birgit.

Elbowing James, Packy chuckled. "See…I tol ya…he likes her…"

James just shoveled another forkful of food into his mouth.

***

BLUE EYES SEARCHED for Birgit, finally spotting her down by the stream, Fritz by her side. Micah headed in that direction.

The dog came to attention as Micah drew near, his tail wagging, causing Birgit to turn her head. Seeing who was approaching her, she returned to focusing on the sunlit burbling stream, ignoring him.

Sitting about six feet from her, he laid back, hands laced under his head, feet crossed and closed his eyes listening to the sounds of the singing water.

A few moments later he said softly, "Friends are hard to find and keep out here, so when we find a goodin', we like to hang on to 'em…"

Birgit's head swiveled at his comment but remained quiet. Micah's deep baritone seemed to reach into her soul with his simple words. She stiffened against the impact.

"We mountain men…ya see…" he continued. "…Are a solitary sort…going months without human contact…"

Birgit frowned, brow crinkling in thought with his words.

Sitting up, Micah pulled a wide blade of grass and placing it between his thumbs, he blew. A warbling shrill sound filled the air making Birgit's scowl go deeper as she stared at him.

He looked intently at her, "Most times we live a lonely existence…much the way I s'pect you be feeling right about now…" he paused, looking for a reaction.

Her stomach gave a lurch at how close his words were to her feelings at the moment. She gazed solemnly at Micah.

"And being way out here…no other woman folk to talk to…well…I reckon it be hard…"

Stretching out, resting on his elbow, head cradled in his hand, while his left fiddled with a blade of grass then pulling it and stuck it in his mouth chewing on it as he gazed at her.

"You're a handsome woman…Miss…"

She blushed at his words, dropping her eyes to stare at her hands in her lap.

"…Any man out here would be proud to call you his wife…"

"Why are you telling me this…?" she asked, looking at him.

Micah shrugged, sitting up again. "Do'no…jus' felt like saying it…"

Miss Birgit's Dilemma: Mail Order Bride

Her gaze drifted over the water to stare at the trees on the other side, noting the deep green of firs and hardwoods.

"Tell me about Johan...what was he like?"

A smile busted out. "Aww...he was a fine 'un...peaceable sort...big, tall kinda like me. But a fine one to have by your side." Micah fell silent remembering his partner.

"You miss him?"

"Aye...I miss him, but life and death is a way of life out here...never know when your last day will be."

"But doesn't that bother you? I mean knowing you might die tomorrow?"

"I try not to think about it too much..." he smiled. "When it's time for the Maker to take me home...won't have a say in the deal."

"Hey...Mick...we's got a barn ta finish up..." Packy yelled.

Smiling again, Micah stood up. "Looks like they need my help..." he began walking up the hill, then coming to a standstill and turning, he addressed Birgit. "It'll be fine Miss..."

"Please let's drop the formalities, Herr Cunningham. Call me Birgit."

"And you call me Micah or Mick as those two lowlifes do...okay?"

Birgit nodded.

Micah turned and strode up the hill, knowing

Birgit's eyes were following every footstep he took, and for some reason that made him happy, adding a spring to his pace.

Chapter Eighteen

A LONE VISITOR stealthy drew closer to the farm with stars his only light; he relied on his nose sniffing the air repeatedly. The ground cushioning every footfall, his body swaying with his weight, the huge grizzly neared the homestead.

Heads sprang up catching a whiff of something on the breeze. The mules began shifting, nervously pawing the ground. Soft bleats became more shrill as the scent of the visitor came closer.

A low growl emitted from Fritz as he bounced up, staring into the blackness at some unseen force. His hackles rose, adding to the already tense feeling in the air.

Some inner warning woke James. Listening, he could hear and feel the fear of the stock as something approached.

Stirring, Micah opened his eyes, automatically feeling the tension. Sitting up and glancing quickly at James he whispered, "The griz…"

James nodded, punching Packy waking him.

"Whaaa…"

"Shush…we's got company…"

Fritz took off after the unseen enemy, frenzied barking fading as he rounded the cabin.

An abrupt roar in defiance of the dog echoed in the dark.

The men grabbed up their rifles and scrambled towards the sound.

Awoken from a deep sleep, Birgit bolted upright in bed, instantly terrified and befuddled as her foggy brain tried to grasp the sounds she heard coming from behind the cabin. All she could pick out was Fritz's growling and frenzied barking. Looking through the window at the night sky, she realized she had forgotten to close them. Hurriedly, she fastened the shutters, placing the cross bar across both windows. Looking at the door, she raced the few feet, and picking up the heavy brace, slipped it into the brackets bolting the door from the inside. She ran back to her bed wrapping the covers around her shivering body and began rocking and silently praying.

Coming to a standstill some twenty feet from the grizzly with Fritz dancing away from the bear's claws then lunging and biting its rump making the bear spin, the three men came to a standstill.

Micah yelled, "Fritz…Fritz…come away!"

The dog ignored him carrying on with his yelping and attacking one who was four times larger than him and probably weighed close to seven hundred pounds.

Miss Birgit's Dilemma: Mail Order Bride

James spoke loudly, "Fan out, if all three of our bullets hit him from different angles, it will at least slow him down."

"Aim ta kill…" added Micah.

Packy inched forward a few feet. Micah and James moved to the right and left, circling in closer for a killing shot.

All three raised their rifles to their shoulders. Flames spitting from muzzle bores lit the darkness. Except for Packy's; his misfired.

Birgit jumped hearing the loud gunfire so close, but remained rooted to the bed too terrified to move.

The grizzly whirled as bullets bit through his hide and blood spurted from the wounds near his shoulders. The bear roared in pain, taking off towards Packy.

"Damn…" he muttered trying to see what had caused the malfunction. Too late, he glanced up as the grizzly was on him in a flash. Knocking him down, the bear ravaged his body, Packy screaming as claws shredded his face and torso. The blood came pouring out of him, staining his clothes and the ground.

When Birgit heard the human sounds of the terror being waged outside, she stuck her fingers in her ears trying to block out the screams. It was no use; she began crying. Crying from fear, fear for the men outside, that they would all die because of her stupidity of insisting on building a home in this ungodly wilderness. She began sobbing hysterically.

His hair ripping from his scalp caused another anguished scream. Mighty teeth gouged into his shoulder as the grizzly picked him up and shook him viciously, snapping Packy's neck and silencing the man's cries abruptly.

Fritz lunged at the bear, who slapped the dog away as if it were a pesky fly. Fritz lay whimpering where he landed several feet away.

As if Packy's lifeless body was now a toy, the monstrous silvertip continued to wreak carnage on the body. Jumping up and down on Packy's torso, the sound of cracking bones mingled with grunts and low growls as teeth gnawed and slashed at the man's clothes and body.

Watching the scene unfold before him, Micah felt helpless as it all happened so quickly. He knew it was too late to save his friend, but he could for damn sure make it so that grizzly wouldn't terrorize this country again.

Tossing his rifle, Micah pulled his knife, circling to the back of the silvertip, which was too busy tearing into the body to take of notice him. He sprang forward, landing on the grizzly's back as it roared, rising and swinging around trying to rid itself of the trespasser. The hilt of the knife gripped tightly in his right hand, his left arm wrapped around the bear's neck in a life or death hold, Micah went for the jugular. Blood spurted covering his hand and arm with warmth and saturated his nostrils with a rich copper smell. The bear roared again fighting with every ounce of strength he had against this human.

James finished reloading, tucking the stock tightly against his shoulder and setting his sights on the chest, he pulled the trigger. Flames flashed, sending a bright light illuminating the ghastly scene.

The silvertip yowled as pain seared his chest giving one last gurgling growl before collapsing to the ground dead, with Micah still on his back.

Dropping the rifle, James rushed to Micah and pulled him away from the grizzly laying him gently in the grass. Running a few yards to the spring, filling the dipper, James returned and handed the now sitting woodsman the water.

Micah drank greedily. He gulped air trying to still his rattling heart. When calm again, he rose to check on Fritz with James following.

Kneeling on one knee, his fingers roaming across Fritz's body, finding nothing but a slight gash in a shoulder, he then gently rubbed the dog's ears. Micah whispered in a voice choked with emotion, "You'll live…boy…you'll live."

Sudden exhaustion had Micah sitting heavily. Hands clasped around his knees he closed his eyes. The events began unfolding in his mind's eye replaying over and over again. He quickly opened them shutting off the visions. Dawn was approaching, carrying that slim line of grey before the sun rose over the horizon. He dreaded what the rising sun would reveal.

"Micah? Packy? James?" a soft voice called from the corner of the porch. "Micah?"

James whispered, "How we gonna tell Miss Birgit?"

Licking dry lips, Micah stood. "She has to know…" he said simply, walking towards the shadowy form in a nightgown with a shawl around her shoulders.

Placing himself between Packy's battered body and Birgit, he grabbed her arms. "Birgit…you need to go back to the cabin."

"Why…?" Then seeing his blood stained hand and shirt, she gasped. "You're hurt!"

"No…I'm fine…Fritz got nicked again, but he's alright."

Birgit looked around Micah's wide shoulder to see Fritz laying his head on someone lying on the ground. Grey eyes grew huge, looking at James and back to Micah. "Packy?"

Micah nodded.

"Nooooo…" she wailed, fighting the woodsman to reach Packy's side.

"Birgit…no!"

"Let me…go!"

"No! Remember him as he used to be…"

Small hands struck Micah's fists and arms holding her, Birgit screamed as tears poured, dripping off her chin, "Packy…" Her hand reaching, wanting to touch him one last time.

Surprised at Birgit's strength from her grief, it took just about everything Micah had to keep her from slipping through his arms. He shouted at James, "Cover him!" he swung Birgit into his arms as she sobbed, still reaching towards the body and crying out "Packy…"

Micah briskly walked back inside the cabin and sat on her bed, rocking and cradling Birgit as one would do a small child. Whispering soothingly in her ear, his fingers gently brushed blonde wisps away from her tear swollen face.

When the sun was high in the sky, Birgit had finally fallen asleep in his arms from sheer exhaustion. Laying her gently on the bed, he stood and covered her. Moving towards the door he turned and gazed at this woman who was beginning to wheedle her way into his heart. But right now he had to make a dirt blanket for a very special man and that, he wasn't looking forward to.

Chapter Nineteen

STANDING OVER PACKY'S grave the two men were silent, wrapped in their own thoughts saying goodbye to a man they both had liked.

Picking up the tools, James told Micah, "Going back down…you coming?"

"I will in a bit…"

"Well…don't tarry too long…we's got work to do…"

Micah nodded.

James turned and trudged off the hill.

Gazing across the vista from where they had laid their friend, Micah knew Packy would enjoy the view.

Turning, he strode far into the dense growth to let loose his grief at the tall trees.

***

THE DAYS STRETCH long and the nights even longer, each one dealing with Packy's death in their own way.

Miss Birgit's Dilemma: Mail Order Bride

The usual lighthearted banter was gone; a weary numbness seemed to shroud their hearts in darkness.

Unable to shake the feeling, they buried themselves in work.

***

UNTYING THE HOBBLES from the milk cow, Birgit led her out of the barn and into the lot. Returning to pick up the bucket of fresh milk, her gaze roamed over the inside of the almost finished structure, remembering Packy's long-winded banter of saying really nothing. Her smile was short-lived as the memories of his tragic death overtook her thought of the fun times with him.

Turning her back on those memories, Birgit stepped into the soon to be heat of the day. Here lately it had not been cooling off at night as it usually did and it was becoming dry, very dry from lack of rain as she gazed at the wilting grasses in the meadow.

Micah met her at the gate, opening and closing it behind her.

"Thank you…"

Nodding, he said casually, "We need rain…if we end up with dry lightning hitting something…we're in trouble."

"What's dry lightning?"

"It's where you have a dry thunderstorm that has hardly any rain with it and produces lightning…"

Ignoring his answer, Birgit blurted out what had

been on her heart since Packy's passing. "I loved him…Micah…" she said softly.

Stopping so abruptly the milk sloshed out of the pail onto his britches, he exclaimed, "What?"

Turning towards him, grey eyes focused intently on Micah as she tried to explain, " I mean…not in the way a woman loves her husband or the way a man loves his wife…but…" she hesitated flicking her gaze away from the woodsman's attentive look.

"…But as a friend, I loved him deeply," she finished, staring at the ground.

"I did too, Birgit…"

She glanced up, squinting against the sun due to his height.

"…Like a brother. He was quirky, odd, a skinny dried up piece of hide, but like Johan, he was one who stood by you no matter what." He glanced around, "Living is hard out here and I can't count on my fingers or toes anymore the friends and brothers I've lost over the years. But I couldn't live any where's else," he said, smiling at her.

Dropping her gaze, Birgit chewed on her bottom lip and stared at the ground.

She started in surprise when a finger touched her chin and gently lifted her face making her look at him.

"Love's a funny word…ain't it? It's only four little letters but it can mean so much…" Micah said, dropping his hand. "…Or so little."

Miss Birgit's Dilemma: Mail Order Bride

Birgit's brow furrowed, taken aback at his insight to the word *love*.

"Here…" handing the pail of fresh milk to her. "Don't want this getting' spoil't." And with that he turned on his heels and walked back towards James where they were working on expanding the field.

Chapter Twenty

STANDING AT THE spring and hearing a hawk's mournful cry, Birgit looked up at the cloudless sky, following its flight as the creature's shadow marked the ground, then the stream, before it flew out of sight. Staring at the grasses she had hoped to use for winter feed, they now lay dead and dried from the sun and heat. Her small garden was only surviving because she watered it twice a day carrying bucket after bucket. Micah had mentioned to her that it had been a long time since he'd seen the woods this dry and told her to pray for rain. She had and continued to pray for rain and many other things, mostly to give her strength to cope in this new land.

Glancing at the men, stripped bare to the waist due to the heat, Birgit knew some icy water from the spring would be welcomed. Kneeling and taking the dipper, she filled it and drank, savoring the cold slipping past her tongue and winding its way into her stomach leaving a refreshing feeling on such a hot day. Fritz joined her, lapping greedily from the small pool. She filled the bucket, picked up the dipper and stood. Gathering her skirts in one hand she made her way towards James and Micah with Fritz following on her heels.

Glancing at the sky she frowned, puzzled by the sudden appearance of dark grey clouds building and wondered where they had come from. "Oh…Lord, yes! Please let it rain!" Her step became a little lighter at the thought of moisture falling from the heavens to quench the thirsty ground.

Her steps slowed to a crawl as she advanced towards the two men working on filling the cracks between logs with mud. Birgit's breath caught softly in her throat as her eyes kept being drawn to Micah with his broad shoulders, thick arms and large hands. Memories flooded her mind remembering the strength of those arms and yet his gentleness of wiping her tears and soft voice consoling her after losing Packy. Tossing those thoughts aside, Birgit swallowed and then licked dry lips preparing to speak.

Feeling something sniffling his leg, Micah looked down; it was Fritz. "Hey boy…" he greeted the dog. "Where's your Mistress…"

"Right here…"

James and Micah looked over their shoulders at Birgit standing several feet away with a bucket and the dipper.

"I thought you might like something cool to drink…" she answered, stepping forward closing the distance between them.

James eagerly grabbed the dipper in his muddy hand saying, "Thankee, Miss Birgit…it's mighty welcomed." He drank deeply and then filled it again, passing the utensil to Micah for his share.

After quenching their thirst, James and Micah leaned against the logs in the scant shade provided by the overhang, resting a bit.

Setting the bucket down, Birgit placed hands on her hips and studied their work.

Noting that, James offered up, "Not much more, Miss Birgit…"

She glanced at him.

"Finish plasterin' the inside and it will be good for whatever thunderous winter God may throw…" he finished.

"Well…I know one thing…" Micah began.

James shot him a look and waited.

Her eyes shifted to Micah.

"…Sure am glad you cut my hair and made me shave my beard off with this heat…" he teased, guzzling another dipperful of water as blue eyes twinkled over the rim at her.

James chuckled softly.

Blushing, Birgit dropped her gaze briefly then raised her chin, tilting her head and eyeing Micah squarely, she answered, "I like to see the face of whom I be speaking to, Herr Cunningham…"

Raising a brow, Micah wondered, *Back to Herr Cunningham…are we?* he thought. Reminding her,

Miss Birgit's Dilemma: Mail Order Bride

"It's Micah..."

Before she could answer, a low deep rumble filled the air. Then a bone-chilling THWACK interrupted the quiet, making all three jump. Sheep and goats bleated; the cow and calf bellowed. The mules nickered and shuffled nervously in the lot.

The air seemed to crackle with energy.

They hurried away from the barn to stare at the sky.

Crowding in next to Birgit's leg, Fritz growled. "Hush..." Birgit told him, smoothing the raised fur back down. "It's just a storm...bringing rain..."

Micah and James cut each other a sharp glance.

"Don't know 'bout that Miss Birgit..."James answered, nodding towards the stock. "They's mighty nervous wit one clap a thunder and that jolt of ligh'tin..."

"And the wind died..." Micah added simply.

"Yep..."

A frown marked her fair features at the warning tone of their conversation. Birgit looked at the sky turning darker by the second. Clouds as black as billowing smoke reminded her of a house fire she had witnessed once in Minnesota.

A gust of hot wind abruptly smacked them in their faces smothering them in fine dust, billowing out Birgit's skirt exposing her ankles. Coughing, she quickly wrapped the material around her legs to keep it from happening again.

The next blast of wind stayed steady but carried a slight hint of smoke. Micah and James cut a quick look at each other. Spinning, Micah roughly grabbed Birgit's arm pulling her close.

"Oww..."

"Now...you listen to me good..."

Birgit reared back from him encroaching into her space, blinking at the abrupt change in his demeanor.

"...We's got a possible fire bearing down on us...and we's don't have time fer your backtalk!"

Her eyes going huge at Micah's announcement, she flicked a look upwards towards the black clouds hovering over the thick forest growth, then back to him.

Dropping her arms, Micah pointed. "You git on up to the cabin and begin packing whatever you can and follow us down the stream...James 'n me..."

"The stream?" She interrupted. "Jumping to conclusions...aren't you? We don't know for sure if there is a fire or not..."

Butting in, James asked her, "You don't smell smoke on the wind?"

Birgit looked with surprise at him. "From one lightning strike? I think you two are imagining things..." she said, folding her arms in front of her.

Snorting, Micah turned her and gave her a shove. "Now git...we ain't got much time!" Throwing words over his shoulder, "James? See if ya can lasso any of that stock..."

Miss Birgit's Dilemma: Mail Order Bride

Whirling, Birgit argued, "How dare you push me!"

Micah's head swiveled. Stepping closer, he leaned threateningly towards her. "I'll do mor'n push you…iffen ya don't get your arse…movin'…woman!"

Birgit gasped at his implied menace, but continued to stand her ground. "I still think you're crazy…there's no fir…" Yelping, "Eeeek…" as Micah turned her and began marching her forcibly to the cabin, muttering, "Damn…you…Birgit! Shad-up and do as I tell you for once! We hain't got time for your sass…"

"Let me go…you're hurting my arm…"

Abruptly pulling up, he spun Birgit to face him. "You ever seen a forest fire? Where nothing is left but a thick coating of ash and the raw stench of burn? Where no life exists anymore?"

"But…"

"You want us to save your stock…and your hide?"

"But…"

"No buts about it…"

Something fluttered in the air from the corner of her eye, Birgit focused on it exclaiming, "Snow? In this weather…"

Micah looked up. "Hell…woman! That ain't snow! It's ash!"

"Ash?" She still didn't believe Micah about a fire

since there seemed to be no evidence of fire eating trees.

"Yes…dammit…ash! Now…move!" Pushing her once again towards the doorway, then spinning and running, he yelled at James, "Take them to that overhang in the bend of the stream." He waved his arms at the stock, panicking them further. Picking up rope from the panniers, Micah tried to lasso Trouble the goat, who kept dodging and bleating. He gave up, swinging one end of the loop using that as a means to herd them down the hill.

Birgit felt Micah and James had lost their minds watching the fiasco of trying to round up the stock and head them to the stream. As she turned, her nose caught a whiff of something, like an old fire gone cold but much stronger. Birgit peeked around the edge of the cabin wall with eyes going wide in fear as she watched flames engulf the huge trees not a half mile from where she stood. Now she could hear the crackling as the fire ate everything in its path moving in her direction.

Glancing over her shoulder at Micah and James near the water's edge, Birgit heard Micah yell, "Let 'em fend for themselves…I'm going back for Birgit!"

With her heart in her throat and her breathing becoming raspy as the smoke filled air became thicker, Birgit rushed and picked up a blanket, laying it on the table and began tossing whatever her hands touched into it. Tying the four corners together, two hands slid under the makeshift handle and wrestled it off the table, its heaviness a surprise as the bundle hit the dirt floor with metallic clinks. Taking a deep breath of smoky air, Birgit coughed and hoisted the bundle. Clumsily turning, she looked up as a shadow filled the doorway. Micah stepped through and easily lifted the bulky makeshift sack as he took her arm and guided her through the exit.

Eyes watering and biting from the smoke, Birgit looked through the thick ash laden air only to see wild creatures bounding past the cabin in fear heading towards the water. Deer, rabbits, squirrels, raccoons and skunks followed each other racing away from impending death. "Where's Fritz?" her voice alluding to the panic she felt. "And Rocky and Stinky?"

"Down with James..." he answered curtly. Dropping the bundle and pulling his knife, Micah cut a slice of dried venison from the ceiling brace stuffing that into the overflowing blanket. "Grab some of those pelts..." he ordered Birgit. "We're gonna need them."

Taking an armful of furs, Birgit was startled when Micah gripped her elbow in his fingers, their strength biting into her flesh. "Hurry...we've got to make that overhang before the fire gets here."

Sparks and ash continued to rain upon them as she stumbled from Micah's rush to get them to safety, Birgit caught herself, then spun for one last glimpse of her little farm. Almost bursting out in tears, she bit them back knowing crying wouldn't heal the wounds the fire was gouging into her little spread.

Roughly grabbing her again, Micah groused. "Don't look back…remember it as it was…"

Numbly nodding, she remembered him saying something like that when Packy had died, as she picked up her pace. Reaching the edge of the water, she watched Micah step into the shallow watercourse and head to the left.

Noticing Birgit not following, he turned and shouted, "C'mon…we ain't got time to lollygag…"

"My shoes…" she called back.

"What?"

"I'll ruin my shoes…and it's the only pair I have…"

"Take 'em off!"

"I can't…"

"Why?"

"The rocks will cut my feet…"

"Hang the damn…shoes!" Micah's face was livid as he rapidly splashed back to her. "I'll make you a new pair…" as he pulled her into the icy water.

Gasping at water so cold it made her legs hurt, Birgit struggled to keep up with the mountain man. Her soggy skirts dragged and slowed her pace to a crawl. Her arms burdened with carrying and keeping the pelts dry hindered any speedy progress. Stopping to catch her breath, Birgit looked back up the hill to the farm, now exploding into flames. A low sob escaped her throat. *All of us worked so hard...* she thought as tears blurred her vision, as did the smoke.

Suddenly, James was there, lifting the pelts from her arms. "Come along, Miss Birgit…not much further…" he beckoned.

Her fingers grasped and pulled as much of the sopping skirt and petticoats out of the water as she could, but it remained a struggle wading through knee high water after James. Her toes were frozen from the icy brook and had no feeling in them, which made her gate clunky and unsteady across the rock strewn bottom.

Seeing James disappear under a granite overhang, Birgit followed, surprised when she stepped into the small washout with a sandy floor.

James explained. "Normally, this would be filled with water, but due to the drought it's not and lucky for us."

Twisting her wet skirts, Birgit nodded as she tried to wring the water out. Looking around the small space, seeing Rocky and Stinky but no one else, panic rose making her squeak when she asked, "Where's Micah, the stock and Fritz?"

"Oh…he changed his mind and is taking the stock further down and across…hopefully they will make it."

Now chilled to the bone despite the heat, Birgit chattered the words out. "Aarrreee…are ttthey…coming back?"

"Yessum...'n they's better hurry!" Spreading a pelt on the sandy loam, he gestured. "Come sit and get warm."

Birgit did, her shaking fingers barely able to unlace her high-top shoes and pour the water out, setting them aside.

James wrapped another pelt around her shoulders. "Smoke might get bad in here Miss...so's iffen it does, jus' bury your head 'neath that pelt."

"Thank you..." she whispered.

Rocky and Stinky pushed their way under her wet skirts, lying quietly against her. Birgit hardly noticed, her eyes glued to the opening hoping Micah and Fritz would be there soon.

James stood a little ways back from the entrance; he, too, was on the lookout for his friend and the dog.

The roar of the flames and wind rose in such intensity it blocked out all other sounds. Thick smoke filled the small area causing Birgit and James to cough uncontrollably. He motioned as he wrapped a bandana around his nose and mouth, shouting, "Pull your wet skirt over your head...then cover up wit the pelt..."

Red-rimmed, frightened eyes stared back at him.

"...It'll keep the smoke out better..."

Birgit tried to swallow back the terror, but it continued to rise in her throat. She felt as if someone was holding a pillow over her face cutting off her air supply, as she remained frozen.

Miss Birgit's Dilemma: Mail Order Bride

Jumping quickly to her aid, James pulled the wet skirt over her face, then the pelt and pushed her back against the sandstone wall. Then he turned and continued to watch the firestorm blazing around them.

Chapter Twenty-One

STARTLED OUT OF a deep sleep, James wondered what had awoken him as he lay back again, eyes closed, his ears tuned to his surroundings.

Then it dawned on him; all was quiet. The roar of the fire and wind was gone. The perfume of fresh, raw burn and lingering smoke was all that remained. He listened to the softly burbling water in the stillness and something else. Rain.

Abruptly sitting up, James stared into the darkness of the shelter. Besides himself, he only saw one lump lying against the sandy loam. Micah and Fritz had not returned.

His heart gave a lurch at the thought of losing another friend so close after Packy's death. "Damn..." he muttered as he jerked the bandana away from his face.

Standing and taking a few steps, he squatted at the brook's edge, cupping his hands; he scooped water to dampen his thirst. James promptly spit out the bitter, ash tainted liquid.

Lifting his head as he wiped his mouth, James

stared through the stillness to across the stream. It was still dark, but he could make out the smoking skeletons that once were a beautiful forest and his home.

Dropping his eyes, James sighed as he swirled a hand in the dirty water. He knew it would take several days for the water to clear; he wondered if the spring had been affected. They would need water.

"James…" Birgit called to him softly.

He turned.

"Is it over?"

"Yessum…" he replied as he stood and walked over to her holding out his hand.

Taking it Birgit rose, looking around. Her heart plummeted to the soles of her feet.

"Micah and Fritz…?"

"No…Ma'am…they's not back, yet."

Collapsing back to the pelt, she choked back a sob, reaching instead for her damp shoes to put on, hiding the emotions she knew were registering on her face.

Standing by, James watched her silently lace up her shoes, then hold out her hand again for him to help her up.

Taking a deep breath and squaring her shoulders, Birgit walked to the edge of the shelter and gazed at the destruction she saw across the water. A hazy, smoke filled view greeted her along with the sharp pungent aroma of burnt woodlands.

James came alongside. "Kinda hard to look at…them woods was my home."

"Mine, too…" came the soft reply.

Crouching, she gathered water in her cupped hands, preparing to drink. James stopped her actions. "Wouldn't do that Miss Birgit…water hain't fit to drink right, yet…full of ash and debris…tastes kinda like lye soap would," he warned. "Without the suds…"

Nodding, Birgit proceeded to wash her face and hands in the biting cold water instead. Her hot, bloodshot eyes welcomed the soothing coolness as she splashed more liquid on her skin.

Taking the corner of her soot covered apron, Birgit wiped her face as she rose.

"When it gets daylight, we'll go back to the farm…" James told her.

She whirled on him, her emotions raw with the thought of also losing Micah and Fritz on top of her home. "And do what? There is no farm to go back to!"

James remained silent a few moments waiting on the tension to settle down.

"I know, Miss Birgit. But…sometimes animals come back to familiar ground once the danger is over…"

Trying hard not to break down, Birgit apologized, "I'm sorry, James. It's not your fault…I know that. It's just…you all worked so hard to make my dream come true…and I thank you for that…"

"Yessum…"

"…But it appears…" she took a big breath. "It appears nature had other ideas."

"Yessum…"

***

SPLASHING THROUGH THE brook, James carried Birgit. Reaching the water's edge, he set her down on burnt ground. "I'll go back and fetch our things."

Turning, she watched him head back to the little shelter. Then she refocused her eyes on the smoldering ruins of the farm.

Picking up her damp skirts, she slowly walked up the hill, stopping when she was twenty feet from what had been her home.

Birgit wanted to cry, scream, throw something, anything to relieve the deep ache she was experiencing in her chest.

But she couldn't.

The numbing pain was too great. She felt as scarred as the landscape.

Jamming her fist in her mouth to keep from screaming out loud as her mind's eye brought forth happier visions of Fritz and then Micah.

Micah… she thought.

Guilt drove in waves over her body as she realized she had killed two men and her dog because of her foolish dream. Birgit sank to her knees in a grief so deep it took her breath away.

Only then did she sob relentlessly, trying to wash the pain from her body.

Chapter Twenty-Two

SHIFTING THE WORN out chaw from one cheek to the other, Whit Broadbent sent a stream of brown juice sailing over the hitch rail into the street at some unseen target.

Only then did he look up, his eyes going wide at who was stumbling down the hillside on the outskirts of the settlement walking towards Trader Charley's. Throwing words over his shoulder, Broadbent yelled, "Hey…Charley! Come quick…ya gotta see this!"

"Aww…hell…Whit!" Charley groused, coming to stand behind Broadbent, thumbs tucked into the strings of his apron. "Hain't ya got something else ta do 'sides pestering me?"

Plucking at Charley's shirtsleeve, pulling him closer, Whit pointed. "Lookie…up thar…hain't that Lavanier and thet woman that went up to Johan's place?"

Squinting to bring the pair into better focus, Charley stared. Then his eyes widened recognizing the bedraggled twosome. "Well…I'll be horn-swoggled…it is Miss Birgit and James! Where'n the hell did he come from?" leaping over the steps and sprinting towards them, with Broadbent on his heels.

Charley's steps slowed taking in the haggard look of Birgit, hair askewed and the haunted look from her eyes shocking him. Reaching the pair, he began removing the makeshift pack from her shoulders, handing it to Whit.

Directing his questions to James, "What happened? Where's Packy..." looking past them, "And the stock...?"

Slipping the pack from his shoulders, James wearily let it fall to the ground.

"Wildfire...nothin' left of Johan's place...don't know if Mick, the stock or the dog made it to safety..."

"Mick was there?"

"We saw the smoke...but the rain killed it for it got here..." added Whit.

James nodded. "Uh-huh...we was fixing the place up for Miss Birgit...that fire...it was a bad 'un."

"Where's Packy?" Charley asked again.

"He's dead..." James said simply.

"I killed him..." Birgit said softly. "And Micah and Fritz..."

James cut a look at Birgit, frowning.

Charley's eyes popped, as did Whit's.

"What...!"

Shaking his head *no* to Charley and Whit, James

Miss Birgit's Dilemma: Mail Order Bride

offered an explanation.

"Don't pay no mind to Miss Birgit…she's kinda haf out of it. Silvertip got 'im before me 'n Mick could stop him…

Birgit mumbled as if in a trance, "I got them killed…for a silly dream…"

Charley stared at her.

"Mick 'n me figure it was the same grizz that got Johan…"

Whit and Charley shifted their eyes back and forth between James and Birgit.

"Dry light'n' started it all…"

"I killed them…" Birgit repeated softly.

James explained again, "She's exhausted…why she's talkin' outta her head…"

Gently taking her arm, Charley steered Birgit towards the trading post, calling for his squaw. "Nona! Nona…come quick!"

Reaching the edge of the steps, Nona saw Charley gesturing to her.

She hurried to his side taking Birgit's arm, slowly guiding her back to the store and inside for some much needed rest.

Picking up James's pack, Charley stated, "Looks like you could use some food, and a stiff drink."

"Aye…" James nodded. "And sleep…"

Chapter Twenty-Three

SITTING ON A boulder out behind the post, Birgit listened to the quiet sounds, but they did nothing to soothe her soul. The sun, hot and bright, did not warm her. After a week of returning to Sinking Springs, resting and eating Nona's food, she still hadn't been able to relieve the guilt that seemed to hang on to her very being. She knew it was foolish to be carrying that around in her heart, but she couldn't seem to shake the gloom and look on the bright side of things no matter how hard she tried.

Six months ago, she had set out on an adventure to become a bride; then she became a widow before she even got the chance to be wedded to Johan with his untimely death. Smiling faintly, she remembered Packy fondly. The tall, scrawny man with his odd way of speaking, his awkward marriage proposal, defending and guiding her, doing everything she had asked of him. Her mind shifted to Micah making her breath catch at the thought of him; his strength and boldness hewed from living in these mountains. The friends he made and lost on this journey he called life.

Miss Birgit's Dilemma: Mail Order Bride

And now he too, along with Fritz was gone, she knew in her heart they had both died in the wildfire. Lifting her head, Birgit let her gaze roam the rugged terrain with its majestic mountains, home to so few humans, but who were strong and independent and who willingly stayed and carved out their existence, calling this wilderness, home.

She sighed as she stood. Birgit realized with a heavy heart she wasn't cut out for this type of life. God had given her the message loud and clear with everything that had happened at the farm. She knew now what she needed to do as she strode back into the post to talk with Herr Charley.

***

WITH HIS MOUTH puckered and one eye squinted, Charley continued to thoughtfully study the tall woman on the other side of his counter with the sad eyes after she made her announcement.

"You see, Herr Charley…" Birgit explained. "…I had enough goods to bring you and settle up my account…in fact, Packy and I were just discussing when to come to town a few days before…" she hesitated, swallowing, "…before he was killed…" her words trailed off thinking of her friend. She dropped her eyes to gaze at her hands resting on the counter. Closing them, she tried to quell the embarrassment of having to ask for fare to go back to Minnesota. Lifting her head, she squared her shoulders giving him a straightforward look. "I promise to pay back every cent I owe you once I get work back ho…." Birgit stopped. *Home…where is home?* she thought. *This is home…no home is back in Minnesota…but it didn't feel like home there anymore, this felt, oh fiddle…* "Uh…once I get back to Minnesota…" She held her breath waiting on his answer.

Resting his forearms on the counter, Charley leaned forward slightly, lacing his hands together before speaking. "You sure 'bout that, Miss Birgit?"

"About what?"

"Leaving us…"

Startled, Birgit hesitated before answering. "Herr Charley…I made a mistake coming out here…"

"Did you?"

Licking dry lips, she answered, "Yes…I'm not strong enough, or brave enough to…to handle this wilderness…"

Straightening, Charley began walking around his counter, "So…youse just gonna turn tail and run…that it?" as he came to stand in front of her.

Speechless, Birgit stared at him. He was bluntly putting into words what she hadn't been able to express.

Charley squinted at her. "You gonna let a few hiccups make you give up?"

A stubborn chin rose, "Losing Packy and Micah and Fritz were not hiccups! They were life changing…and I'm not giving up…I'm just going back to a

Miss Birgit's Dilemma: Mail Order Bride

life I know…a life that better suits me."

"Uh-huh…youse is running…running scared…plain and simple… 'sides you don't know fer sure Micah is dead."

"Yes, I do…I feel it in my heart," she stubbornly declared. "And…I'm not scared…Herr Charley."

Scratching his head, "Ya…don't say. Could'a fooled me…"

Dropping her eyes, Birgit studied her worn and scuffed toes of her shoes peeking out from under her dress. Looking up, she softly stated, "You don't understand…"

"Oh…I understand…I understand plenty…" Moving around his counter he addressed her from the other side. "I came out here in the thirties…can't tell ya how many times I wanted to give up." He cocked a brow at her. "But I didn't."

Sighing, Birgit told him, "Herr Charley…you can't change my mind…I'm going back…that is if you'll loan me the fare…"

Ignoring her comment, Charley continued, "When ya first came I thought you was loco…but then I saw ya had sand…"

Frowning, she asked, "Sand?"

Handing her a peppermint candy stick, he explained, "Means…ya got grit…courage, determination…"

Taking the stick candy her face puckered in thought. "But I am none of those things…"

Juliette Douglas

Pointing his own candy stick at her, he said, "Yeah, ya 'r...ya jus' don't know it yet..." taking a bite of the peppermint.

Listening to the sounds of teeth crunching the candy, Birgit didn't know what to say at first, finally blurting out, "But I failed..."

"Naw..." Charley grinned. "Ya jus' had a few hiccups...like all of us do now 'n a'gin. This land is growing and we need women like you to help it grow..."

Frown going deeper, Birgit realized this conversation was not going the way she thought it would. "But..."

"...And, sometimes Miss...ya just gotta have a little faith that things will be alright. Now here's the deal...I'll not be giving you a loan..." Charley watched Birgit's face fall to the floor.

"I want you to think real hard on staying...this little stick in tha mud place will grow one day and I'll be needing to sell more goods..." He tilted his head observing Birgit's reaction. "Like butter, eggs...cheese..."

"I don't have the stock anymore..."

"I'll get you more stock..."

"Herr Charley...that's very kind of you, but I can't let you do that for me...I'm indebted to you enough..."

"Now...Miss, you jus' let me worry 'bout thet..." He gazed at her with a twinkle in his eyes. "

Miss Birgit's Dilemma: Mail Order Bride

'Sides…I like you…ya got spunk…"

A faint smile broke out on a weary face. "And suppose…I don't take you up on your offer?"

Charley grinned. "You will…"

Planting hands on her hips, she scolded, "Herr Charley…you drive a hard bargain and are one stubborn man…" And with those words Birgit turned on her toes and marched out the doors to the front porch and down the steps.

He chuckled as he watched her skirts swish through the exit.

Chapter Twenty-Four

TOUCHING THE BARK with her hands, Birgit leaned backwards against them and the solid strength of the tree as she gazed at the majestic mountains that reminded her so much of her native Sweden. Smiling, she watched Rocky and Stinky scamper about between rocks and bushes in amongst the trees, playing. Lifting her head, grey eyes once again roamed the peaks, but a few moments later that scene blurred then faded as pictures of past images from her mind's eye came forth. Arriving in Sinking Springs, Packy fighting so gallantly for her against the despicable Randall. Herr Charley's bluster opposing her plan, but finally relenting and getting the stock she required and Packy guiding her to Johan's home. A faint smile bloomed thinking of the tall burly woodsman, Micah and the verbal battles they had exchanged. That smiled faded as she remembered James saying Micah was downstream trying to save the stock from the fire as she and James took shelter in a small washout. Birgit blinked rapidly trying to quell the tears that threatened to overflow. Two good men and her dog,

Miss Birgit's Dilemma: Mail Order Bride

Fritz had died at her expense and she wasn't sure she could go through that again.

Birgit wondered if she should make her stand in this rough and tumble land or run, run scared as Herr Charley said she wanted to do. Micah was right; it was a hard land and only the strong would survive to settle this wilderness and she wasn't sure she was up to the task.

If she decided to take Herr Charley up on his offer, she and Nona would be the only women in Sinking Springs. Birgit didn't like the feeling of being fair game to the men in the small community, though she knew the shop keep and James would protect her. Lord help her if Randall tried to accost her again.

Giving a long sigh, Birgit pushed herself away from the tree and picking up her skirts, she began the trek up the incline to her favorite perch to have a heart to heart with God. He would know what she should do.

Chapter Twenty-Five

REACHING THE OUTSKIRTS of Sinking Springs, Micah sighed with relief. Herding stock with brains no bigger then a pine nut had to be the hardest job he had ever tackled. Logging, trapping, hunting was easy compared to trying to corral Birgit's farm critters.

Birgit... he thought. It dawned on him that he was anxious to see her and find out if she was okay, *...and James, too, of course.*

But his mind lingered on the tall blonde woman whose spunk, determination and crazy ideas had angered him at first. Eventually, though, he came to admire her for being and thinking differently.

The stock headed off to his right into a semi-sheltered meadow; Micah knew they would be okay there for a few hours. Calling to Fritz, the two of them traveled down a lonesome street, not a soul in sight as he reined up in front of Trader Charley's. Sliding wearily off the back of the mule, Micah threw the rope reins over the hitch rail as he climbed the steps.

When a shadow caught the corner of his eye,

Miss Birgit's Dilemma: Mail Order Bride

Charley's mouth dropped a mile as he looked up and saw Micah walking towards him. "Well...I'll be horn-swoggled... Where'n the hell did you come from...Mick?"

Sitting gingerly on the one stool in front of the counter, Micah replied tiredly, "Don't ask..."

Fritz settled upon the planked floor by the woodsman's feet, letting loose a long sigh himself and closing his eyes.

Chuckling at Micah's reply, the shop keep reached under the counter and pulled a bottle out, turned and plucked a tin cup from behind him. The cork squeaked as he twisted it out of the bottle, pouring a generous amount of amber liquid in the cup and sliding it towards Micah.

Nodding his thanks, Micah picked it up and drank greedily, enjoying the warmth hitting his empty stomach. Dropping his head, he burped silently.

Resting his forearms on the counter, Charley leaned across closer to Micah and asked, "Fire a bad 'un? We saw the smoke just a billowing outta them mountains, but then the rains came...t'weren't sure you would make it out..."

Micah nodded.

"James and tha Miss came in a little over a week ago..."

Micah's head snapped up. "She okay?"

Puckering his lips, Charley replied, "Uh-huh...but she thinks you're dead along with Fritz..."

"What?"

"Been a mite upset about it, too…thinkin' of leaving…goin' back to…um…Minnesota…" he cocked a brow at Micah waiting on his reaction.

"No! She can't!" Realizing too late what he blurted out.

The other brow cocked while Charley kept his face deadpanned as his eyes twinkled.

Clearing his throat, Micah asked, "Uh…where is Birgit…"

"Well…now le'me see…" he began by pulling his watch out of his trousers pocket and popping the case open, pretending to study the time.

Slamming his fist on the counter, Micah rose threateningly and hissed, "Dammit…Charley! Where is she?"

Fritz rose and waited expectantly.

"Hang on…I'm gittin' to it…now it's four twenty and 'bout this time…ev'ry day…she goes for a walk…"

"Where?"

Charley pointed towards the rear of the store. "Out…"

Micah and Fritz rushed and disappeared through the back door together.

"…There somewhere's…" he said to the air in an empty room.

Chapter Twenty-Six

CONCENTRATING, BLUE EYES darted everywhere, around trees, brush and small boulders, searching for Birgit as Micah continued walking up the rise. Fritz bounded away from his side; he smiled knowing the dog had caught wind of her. Topping the long hill, he quietly watched the reunion between Birgit and Fritz.

Jumping as something nudged her elbow, Birgit turned her head and gave a short cry at seeing Fritz. Grasping his face in her hands, she began kissing the dog about his head and ears. "Oh…Fritz…you made it!" Gently, her fingers roamed his body looking for burns, abrasions. When she found none, Birgit knelt in front of him and took him in her arms, wetting his fur as tears of relief spilled over at his return.

Micah crept closer, watching this strong woman who had worked so hard to make her dream come true. He knew now that he wanted Birgit by his side always, building not only hers, but their own dreams together.

"Oh…Fritz…I wish Micah had made it out, too…"

"I did."

Birgit gasped as her head swiveled seeing the tall woodsman.

"And so did the stock…"

Rising slowly, speechless, Birgit gulped air back into her deflated lungs at the astonishing sight of seeing Micah standing there, disheveled and worn, but there, nonetheless.

He grinned, "Well…you glad to see me…or not?"

Picking up her skirts, she ran to him throwing her arms around his neck with such force he almost lost his balance as more tears fell.

"Whoa…now…I'm all right…no need to fret…" holding her tightly, his heart singing at her response.

"I…I thought you were dead…" she sniffled against his neck, her nose registering his masculine scent mingled with smoke and sweat from his ordeal. But she didn't care as she clung to him just glad to have her arms around his warm and breathing body.

"So…Charley said…" gently pushing her back as he gazed at her. His thumbs tenderly wiping the tears dripping off her chin only to have others take their place. "Now…now…enough tears…"

Nodding, Birgit hastily brushed them away, sniffling in the process, taking the corner of her apron and wiping her nose with it.

Miss Birgit's Dilemma: Mail Order Bride

"The stock is safe, I'm safe and so is Fritz…don't think the chickens made it, though…"

Still speechless, all Birgit could do was nod again.

"…But we can get more, and go back up there and rebuild or find a new place with more pastureland…" Tilting his head, Micah waited on her response adding, "That is if you are planning on staying…"

Her mouth dropped open, grey eyes wide. "Who told you I was thinking of leaving?"

Looking at the sun beginning to show off its evening colors, Micah answered, "Oh…some cantankerous old bird…"

"Herr…Charley?"

"Uh-huh…"

"Oh…Micah…I didn't know what to do. I felt so guilty about Packy and then when James and I arrived and you and Fritz…" she trailed off her eyes searching his, for what she didn't know.

Resting his big palms on her shoulders, he reassured her. "It's okay…"

Feeling the weight of his hands gave her confidence. She stepped into his arms again, her hands sliding up his back feeling the muscles ripple at her touch; Birgit's words became muffled by his shirt. "I don't want to lose you again, Micah."

Enjoying the feel of her hands on his back Micah was surprised at her words. Pushing her back, he grinned. "Whoa…now…is that a proposal?"

Blushing, Birgit focused on the funny looking necklace still around his neck for a few moments before looking up and blurting out, "I love you, Micah."

Dropping his hands from her shoulders, he scratched his head and pretended to ponder her words. Turning away, Micah walked a few feet, then whirled about, facing Birgit, noticing how she anxiously awaited his reply. "Well…now, le'me think about this for a bit…"

Birgit's heart fell to her toes, but that stubborn chin rose as she spoke forcefully, "If ye be thinking of me as a kept woman…Herr Cunningham…ye better think again…!" Folding her arms across in front of her as she glared at him.

Micah blinked not expecting that. "Now…you just hold on…dad-gummit!" he flared. "You hardheaded, contrary dad-gum female! I'll wear the britches in this family!"

Birgit gasped.

Striding towards her, he grabbed her upper arms. "And I'll be the one astin' the marrying question!"

Grey eyes grew round as wheel hubs.

His eyes straying to her lips, Micah remembered the last time he'd stolen a kiss from her, when Spotted Wolf had visited them to warn about the grizzly. He wanted to taste them again, *now*. Pulling her in close, his head lowered as he lightly brushed her lips with his own. When she didn't resist, he deepened the kiss, tasting her.

Birgit melted into his body, wrapping her arms around Micah's neck returning his kisses with urgent ones of her own.

Fritz not understanding his humans, began barking, finally standing on his back legs pawing at Micah's arms, breaking the two apart.

Chuckling, Micah told the dog, "Boy…better get use to it…"

Giggling, Birgit touched lean cheeks. "I love you, Micah."

Grinning, he replied, "I love you, too…though it took me a while to figure it out…had a lot of time to think, herding your contrary stock to safety."

Smiling, Birgit told him, "Kiss me again…Micah…"

"Yessum…"

***

December 1857

DARKNESS HAD FALLEN in Sinking Springs. Birgit stood at the one window she had insisted on Micah putting in when he and James had built a temporary home for them as they decided on what to do next. She watched the big flakes fall silently as she sighed happily. Her hand slid to her tummy where a tiny human was taking shape. Birgit was only two and a half, maybe three months along but she loved the fact she was carrying Micah's child. *Their child they had made together through their love.*

The sharp scent of the fir in the corner of the room thrilled her. This Christmas would be the best one since she came to America. Tomorrow, the whole settlement was converging on Herr Charley's for a Christmas dinner, something she knew she would enjoy.

Looking up from the book he was reading, Micah gazed tenderly at his wife. He smiled thinking of the spats they still had, but it seemed to have drawn them closer and he had to admit that sometimes Birgit was right.

Standing and laying the book in his chair, Micah walked over to his wife, wrapping arms around her and nuzzling her neck.

Birgit leaned back against his solid frame, relishing the security and contentment it gave her.

"When do you think the wee one will get here?"

"Spring."

"Wonder if it will be a girl…with fire and brimstone like her Mother?"

Turning in his arms, her hand tenderly touched the face she loved. "No…it will be a boy…strong and fearless like his Father…"

Micah grinned. "Ya think so…?"

"I know…so"

Miss Birgit's Dilemma: Mail Order Bride

"Hum…"
"Kiss me Micah…"
"Yessum…"

THE END

About the Author

Author Juliette Douglas is shown with white thoroughbred stallion Arctic Bright View who played **'Silver'** in the 2013 remake of **The Lone Ranger**.

Both hail from Marshall County, Kentucky.

Photo by Lois Cunningham, Benton, KY

Visit our websites:
http://juliettedouglas2016.wix.com/mysite
www.megsonfarms.com

Visit Juliette Douglas via Facebook:
www.facebook.com/author.juliette.douglas

SADDLE UP... LET'S RIDE!

Made in the USA
Lexington, KY
22 March 2017